MW00974598

The Stories of Goom'pa: Book 1

Goom'pa and Shine

by Vikrant Malhotra
illustrated by Rachael Mahaffey

Copyright © 2014 Vikrant Malhotra
All rights reserved.

ISBN: 061598505X
ISBN 13: 9780615985053
Library of Congress Control Number: 2014935619
Istara Creations, Delray Beach, FL

This book is dedicated to my mother, Kanchan

TABLE OF CONTENTS

ACKNOWLEDGMENTS

Victoria –

This book would not have happened without you coming into my life. I told you silly stories and you encouraged me to put pen to paper. You listened and lovingly assisted with the edits and revisions and saw me through all the rock and roll as the journey unfolded. You picked up the pieces as I stumbled down the path which brings us to this juncture. The tale has been written. I offer it up to my audience hoping it will romance them, as it did you.

1

THE SEARCH

More quickly than the eye could follow, the Ancient, Zydaar, shot across the infinite vacuum of space. Arms held closely to his superbly muscled and bejeweled body, he traversed the endless void. With Zydaar a thousand times faster than a hurtling comet, even star beams dared not chase him.

As if he were unfolding giant sails, Zydaar slowly spread his radiant wings open to their full expanse. With a powerful incantation, he turned those wings into enormous mirrors that reflected all parts of the kingdoms he flew by.

Any region of the empire that caught Shine's attention was magnified by the light of Zydaar's wings. The angel helped Shine focus on even the most remote part of the universe she desired to view.

What shall bring the smile back to this sweet child's face? Zydaar wondered. As Shine's guardian, he was determined to restore her good cheer. Trust had been bestowed on him by Shine Star when she expressed her loneliness.

✳ ✳ ✳

"To your left," she called out to Zydaar, from her vantage point far away in the heavens. Her instincts guided Zydaar as he passed countless galaxies and colorful formations. Shine scanned them all with great intent, her feelings acting as his compass.

She focused, probing the constellations and studying each star and comet.

What was she hoping to find with the Ancient's help? The young star experienced both hope and despair as her pulse quickened.

Zydaar soared, painting the night with rainbow lights and chasing after Shine's line of sight.

Far and away, she picked up on a remote galaxy named the Milky Way.

What was so unusual about this place? Something about this sector of the boundless cosmos tugged at her soul. "Please wait, guardian!"

Casting mystical rays, Zydaar hovered over the region.

"Do you spot that star? I believe it's named Sun." Shine's concentration increased as her heart raced with anticipation. "Ah, Sun has many planets twirling around it! The third planet is Earth." Shine fought to contain her excitement.

The angel circled over the globe, zooming in on details so Shine might survey them with clarity.

"Why, thank you, beloved guardian. My heart gives strength to sight. I can zero in now and sense a mysterious vibration from this place."

Concentrating fixedly, her vision reached ever deeper into the night side of Earth.

Someone hid in the forest, a presence in an area where the woods appeared green, even in the blackness.

Careful! Zydaar chided himself. Had he been seen? In haste, he folded his wings and used a magic charm to turn invisible.

To an observer on Earth, Shine was a remote star twinkling in the far, distant sky.

✳ ✳ ✳

As she stilled her mind, her perception expanded, and her sight became ever sharper.

Searching...

Her starlight fell as silken threads on the land.

"There! Behind that bush, who hides yonder?" She sensed emotions. Surely the being was no more than three inches high. Who might it be? Catching her breath, she sighted a glint.

"What kind of light is that?" Her heart raced; her image was reflected back from the eye of a miniscule creature.

How small he was. She twinkled in astonishment.

The tiny body hid behind a leaf, looking directly at her. He sneaked a shy look, showing only one eye.

Oh, dear. She breathed hard, knowing a stirring, deep and forceful. A shower of sparks exploded from her being.

The creature blinked and continued to peek at her. With effort, Shine tried to glance away, yet she couldn't. The shy, fragile soul called to her essence as he hid and studied her.

His name was Goom'pa. He was a resident of Palidon, the Small Animal Kingdom.

As Shine pulsed with tenderness, her light reached out to the small being below. "Are you the one who pulls at my core?"

The curious little soul was furry and stinky.

Zydaar's brow furrowed into a frown as he examined the puny fellow.

"This thing, it's no bigger than a human thumb." Sensing that it peeped at Shine, the angel felt his age and smiled.

"Tiny creature, dare you to stare at the princess?" The Ancient shook his mighty head.

Good grief, this elfin spirit suffered with yearning for the king's daughter. *Ye gods, much trouble in the heavens shall follow this,* he groaned.

And yet, Goom'pa kept on gazing at the beautiful light. With delicate paws, he held on tightly to the leaf he hid behind. One eye reflected her back at the starlit cosmos.

"Groo, groo, groo..." he grunted. He held much hope within his heart.

"Groo...!"

The young star had stumbled upon the one she searched for. And thus she discovered the feelings Goom'pa had for her, Prime Ray's daughter.

As he flew back home, Zydaar reminisced about the events leading up to the search. It had all started thousands of years before...

2

SHINE STAR

The Ancient reached back in time to that fateful day.

The heavens rested peacefully. The stars blazed, filling the infinite universe with dancing lights. Master of the universe Prime Ray felt the delight of his kingdoms. Comprising endless faraway lands and empires, creation was his to command.

With Prime Ray in charge of the manifest world, the galaxies, planets, and moons, all fell under his sway. Managing both the young and the old, the big and the small stars, he reigned sovereign above them all.

He prevailed over Star Lords, the mighty powers that oversaw vast regions of space. Ministering to baby stars, just growing and learning how to shine, Prime Ray protected and guided their development. He further regulated the angels, guardians, and other miraculous entities and gave them direction.

The radiance of Prime Ray, the supreme ruler, a wise and loving king, could be seen by the entire realm. Under his authority, they lived content. At least, most did.

✳ ✳ ✳

My beautiful lands! His gaze swept over the vast expanse of space, sending out bursts of joy.

Look how radiant were his stars! Pulsing with pride, he blessed them all. A million shining lights twinkled back in response. All of eternity sensed his ecstasy. Shooting stars crisscrossed the endless blue.

In that instant, Prime Ray was overcome with bliss. Unable to contain his happiness, he poured forth rays of a thousand colors.

One of his twinkles took on a dazzling radiance of its own. With giggles and peals of laughter, she started to spin and raced as fast as light, exploring her newfound universe...

Perfect and pure of form, a baby star had been birthed.

She emerged as innocent as any newborn. When she zoomed through the trillions of galaxies, a peaceful spot caught her fancy, and she settled in.

The party of starbursts and sparkles came to a standstill. In awe, millions of heavenly beings paused.

Prime roared with joy. Intense bursts of light exploded from his core.

Shine Star, princess of the universe, was the most precious and rare of all creations. As an expression of perfect happiness, thus was the king's daughter born.

Soaring through space, Zydaar continued to sort through his memories.

3

SHINE STAR—A FEELING

Thousands of years passed.

In time, Shine grew brighter, ever more beautiful.

Watching her play and laugh brought the king joy and a sense of contentment he hadn't known before.

Over the millennia, many celestial bodies, including Star Lords, arrived to pay their respects. Heavenly beings sang Shine's praises; armies of angels offered prayers.

Delighted by the fascinating displays of affection and colorful ceremonies, the princess would squeal with joy.

Dancing with the angels and frolicking with the stars, she played all kinds of games that the guests invented to amuse her.

And yet, after a while, her sparkle dimmed.

Despite Prime Ray's love, and the countless caring admirers, something was amiss.

Feeling somber, Shine stopped the game of spins she had been playing with colorful spirits recently arrived from far away.

She sighed.

"What troubles our princess?" probed the Golden Angel.

"Is there a matter of concern?" queried the Yellow Spirit.

"Oh, precious Shine, what's on thy mind?" A shooting star called as it raced by.

"Gracious and divine souls, you are ever so kind. The wonderful and choice gifts you bring me—rainbows and stardust and sparkles. I'm grateful for your many blessings." She twinkled at her playmates.

However, she didn't express her loneliness.

"Young one, do this aging warrior a favor." So spoke Zydaar. At Shine's side since the day she was born, the angel's love and loyalty were boundless.

A true Ancient One, he was countless years old, timeless and immortal. Created from magic and star beams, he had one function and one duty: to protect her.

As a member of the Crystal Circle, he had absolute authority to fulfill her every wish. These powerful angels reported directly to the king and performed numerous mystical deeds to help run the many kingdoms.

The Ancient's handsome body was spun of blue, green, and yellow glints. Crystal wings carried him beyond the far realms faster than even light could travel. Those wings were richly interwoven with delicate patterns of silver and gold.

Using powerful magic, Zydaar moved too swiftly for the human eye to see.

✳ ✳ ✳

"Precious child, speak your heart." Folding intricate wings, he floated up before his ward.

He gazed at her with devotion, pearly white eyes swirling like galaxies. A thousand questions raced through his mind.

"Beloved Zydaar, teacher and guide, do not regard me so seriously! It's just that..." She glanced away.

Ever patient, he remained suspended in the blackness of space. Slowly, she turned to look at her protector, resting silver rays on his powerful shoulders.

"Jewel of our lord, Prime Ray, tell me, sweet child, do you have less than complete bliss in your life? Clearly, I sense an unfulfilled desire. How can I help?"

She sent waves of love to her friends and well-wishers, who attended her always. Respecting her need for privacy, they withdrew.

"Stay, Zydaar. Let us speak. Do I have my sire's affection?" The shine of Shine's many shining rays diminished.

"Young one, you were created of his boundless happiness. All the riches of these infinite lands are yours to command." Zydaar fluttered his wings across sweeping panoramas of stars and constellations.

The princess sighed. "Countless wondrous entities visit me from faraway kingdoms. I get to play with everyone and lack for nothing. And yet, I am alone."

The angel's frame trembled; giving out a shower of diamond sparks. Created before time, he had observed many events.

He had been present in the remote past when Prime Ray exploded into life from a swirling ball of lightning. The Ancient had witnessed Shine's maker come into his full powers, then his rise to become king of the universe.

Now, his instincts caused him concern.

"What do you want for? Don't you have all of heaven to amuse yourself with?"

"I believe the question is 'who' I'm lonely for. How do I fill this void in my heart?" Her rays dimmed so low that darkness almost set in.

Every fiber in the Ancient's body longed to find a solution to Shine's pain.

Thus began the long, long search. And the discovery of Goom'pa!

As he journeyed the endless distance to his home, Zydaar returned his attention to the present. *I'm at a loss! How is this strange thing going to play out? Who is this creature the princess so desires, and what is known about his lands?* Head full of questions, he flew through the night.

4

PRIME RAY—THE COMMUNICATION

On planet Earth, at the southern edge of Miron National Forest existed the lands of Palidon, a mystical region into which no human had ever crossed.

Strong wizardry ensured outsiders who came too close would feel confused and disoriented and change their mind about entering the jungle.

The Magic Bubble surrounding this kingdom was woven by the Elanian fairies. When called upon, they formed a circle around this abode of many small creatures. As one, they sang a magical spell, creating a sphere of protection over this region where numerous souls lived in harmony. Most were blissfully ignorant of the outside world.

Over time, Palidon became precious to those in the heavens.

The events that led to the shielding of this realm were a story that involved twists and turns known only to a select few.

And it all started with Prime Ray.

✳ ✳ ✳

Prime Ray didn't take for granted the incredible beauty and magnificence of the kingdoms he ruled. As king, he oversaw and commanded mighty Star Lords and unlimited forces. Often, conflict proved unavoidable, and on occasion war erupted among the willful chiefs.

Not all affairs could be maintained or carried out in a completely orderly fashion when one supervised a celestial ocean so far reaching. The considerations of forceful lords and countless gentle inhabitants had to be weighed and carefully balanced.

The territories paid allegiance to Prime Ray. However, powerful energies under his rule were often headstrong. As emperor, he thought a great deal about how to govern well.

Most lords and chiefs showed complete loyalty to him. Others were not always so agreeable. Strong leaders, they didn't submit easily to an overlord. On the other hand, they paid heed to the powers and forces the king commanded. Thus, peace and order most often prevailed. All respected the wisdom of his authority, though some were grudging in accepting oversight.

In addition to loyal stars, Prime Ray had potent energies and legions of magical entities at his call. An army of angels and supernatural forces were his to command. Their numbers were massive and of several kinds. The Ancient Ones, the Crystal Circle, stood strong beside him. Zydaar ranked among the wisest in this sacred chamber.

By exercising both sound judgment and might, the emperor commanded respect and maintained amity between the powers in the universe.

To a large degree, he succeeded.

He had come to appreciate a long time ago that a greater intelligence than even he had created the infinite. He struggled to remember this mysterious presence, but a barrier existed to some memories.

One day, he had just finished sorting out a major clash involving the fierce lords, Rath and Ba'raan. Both desired the same prize, the Milky Way. Of the two, Rath received full control of the galaxy. In exchange Ba'raan was awarded Andromeda, a constellation of many bright stars.

An uneasy truce reigned once more.

Prime Ray sat back on his Throne of Crystals and took a deep breath. This argument between the two could have gotten ugly. A battle involving these strong chiefs would have wreaked unspeakable destruction and disturbed the balance of power within the empire.

The king thus pondered his hard-fought success in fending off a confrontation that might have pitted a merciless Rath against the equally fierce Ba'raan.

Absorbed in his thoughts, he was startled when a commanding voice rang out in his mind. "You are my idea brought to life, Prime Ray!" Clear as glass, the message came through. Though gentle, yet the thought was strong—firm but kind.

"With supreme authority comes much responsibility. Thus, you have been granted the gift and charge of maintaining peace in all of creation.

"This universe was birthed for a profound reason."

Eyes closed, Prime Ray calmed his senses, taking in the information.

"Your immense task is to command and run this vast cosmos for the highest of causes. To create a kingdom where love and innocence are protected and grow. These are the most sacred blessings I can bestow on my children—all that exists.

"Remember this, and you shall fulfill thy function!"

The king looked around, startled.

The voice was gone.

Had he imagined the presence? Had an intelligence actually reached out to him?

Was it my imagination? No. He remembered being surrounded by strength and tenderness.

The communication was pure and true. He reflected on his duties, defined in simple yet quite clear terms.

An idea arose.

He shifted his attention and gazed far into the beyond.

Ahh! He smiled. Love's song could be heard across paradise in diverse and enchanting ways, if one but listened.

In the distance, Prime Ray sensed a vibration from a distant formation, the Milky Way. This seemingly ordinary galaxy had been the motive for the feud between his two dominant lords.

Hmm, strange that this region should catch my attention again, he mused, focusing in on the yellow star, Sun. This particular solar system had multiple planets, including one called Earth.

Something caught Prime Ray's interest, a wooded area on Earth.

Hmmm... He peered at this little globe, concentrating intently on Palidon.

Fragile creatures lived in these jungles. Rich emotions coursed through their souls.

How could these tiny animals have such complex feelings and passion? *They, the inhabitants, don't even seem particularly smart.* The king wasn't sure why he sensed them to be special. He felt urgency that this untouched realm required protection.

The innocence of this land needed to be maintained. For reasons he didn't yet fathom, he knew this would prove important for all. But guarding the forest so far away might not prove quite that easy.

＊ ＊ ＊

5

PALIDON - THE PROTECTION

The Milky Way and a thousand surrounding galaxies and formations existed under the control of Rath. He had emerged as the formidable Red Giant. Millions of stars in this vast region owed allegiance to him, including Sun.

Powerful entities such as Rath had placed themselves under Prime Ray's dominance. Prime Ray knew that one did not maintain control over these massive egos by showing them disrespect or being dismissive. The king used care and judgment in his dealings with the chiefs.

The red star shone strong; raging fires and veins of black clouds circled his gigantic form.

"Rath, I desire your attention on a subject of some importance," Prime communicated on beams of light.

The Star Lord heard the message and focused his powers on the distant but mighty king. "Prime Ray, always such a pleasure to have your company!" Fiery sparks exploded from Rath's massive frame. "Pray tell, what weighs on the heart? We are pleased with our new command of the Milky Way, which Ba'raan dared to eye."

Prime Ray let out a powerful laugh, sending comets shooting across vast distances. "Oh, do be humble in this moment of victory. You have done well for yourself! But let me state my case," the king continued.

"There is a star in your galaxy, Sun, and the system he controls has many planets. One is called Earth. On this land is a

kingdom of little creatures. I desire it be granted exclusive protection from forces I deem intrusive."

Prime Ray paused. Then he went on, "We appeal to your
generosity. Allow me to send in the Elanians to weave a magic
bubble to surround this area. Further, I ask you to assign a Grand
Protector to oversee the souls that live in this domain."

Was this a trick of some kind? Rath was bemused. He looked
across black space, toward Earth, zooming in on the little
kingdom.

*Hmm, pint-size creatures...*Rath became aware of them. The
giant furrowed his brow and concentrated further on the forest.

Rath felt a temptation to deny the request, but he couldn't
come up with a good enough reason to risk confrontation.

Plus, he found himself in a particularly fine mood.

The emperor had allowed him to take the Milky Way as his
prize. Yes, Ba'raan got Andromeda. Nevertheless, the ambitious
chief had received his object of desire in the bargain.

A thoughtful silence ensued as Rath reviewed the situation.
The king waited patiently.

What are the stakes? Rath pondered, not picking up on any
plot that might be to the other's advantage.

There's something about this place I can't quite put a finger on,
he mused.

"Prime, you seem to ask for little," he growled at last. "I shall
grant the appeal. My lieutenant, Mauroga, is to be assigned for
oversight of these...uh, creatures! Further, the Elanian fairies
may weave their magic on this kingdom. They need, however, to
be monitored as per protocol."

The king shone strongly on him, conveying gratitude.

"But, it should be noted," boomed out Rath. "The spell cannot be unlimited in strength. The forces must be balanced in my regions of authority." The Red Giant overflowed with forceful eruptions, pouring out flames that arced over the emptiness.

"Free will shall have its place. For reasons I cannot fathom, you care deeply for these souls. Should they fall into trouble of their own making and not caused by an external force, there can be no interference in their affairs," Rath thus spoke firmly.

The king sighed. Such were the deals and bargains he struck.

"Agreed, I give my word to you. Royal authority will not be exercised in this region without limits. Please accept my gratitude." He shone with satisfaction.

As a result, Palidon came to endure the passing of years.

At the time Prime struck the deal with Rath, he hadn't planned on Shine Star's birth. With all his foresight, he couldn't have anticipated her search—or her reaction upon finding Goom'pa.

6

GOOM'PA AND D'UH!

Ancient One, Purple Angel, and lieutenant to Rath, Mauroga rested high up on the limb of a jacaranda tree. The Ancient had changed form to become a part of this animal kingdom on Earth. The jaguar's silken, dark coat was completely invisible to the casual observer.

"Grrr...," he rumbled in quiet tones, lazily stretching his massive paws.

Peering into the blackness, he sniffed the jungle scents. The cat possessed an acute sense of smell and hearing and monitored for anything unusual.

Mauroga didn't pick up any unrest in the forest this evening. Ever on guard, he remained vigilant. This was his function.

Upon receiving instructions from Rath, he'd used his considerable powers of magic to descend to Earth. Casting a spell, he transformed into the Jaguar, Grand Protector of Palidon. This transition followed Prime Ray's arrangement with Mauroga's lord to grant select protection to this unique land. The negotiation had taken place thousands of years before.

Bound by a directive from his Star Lord, Mauroga knew the elfin creatures, the Poofys, were his to guard and protect. An eternal spirit, he watched countless tales play out in this region.

Over eons and ages, the Poofys had lived under Mauroga's protective presence. Mauroga had witnessed the cycle of their birth and life stories through the ages. And over this considerable expanse of history, with some reluctance, he'd developed a genuine fondness for them.

Were someone to suggest he had a soft spot for the little ones, he would roar and bare his mighty fangs. None dared upset Mauroga! While never openly acknowledging affection, if he suspected them vulnerable to the slightest harm, Mauroga's reaction came fierce and swift.

✳ ✳ ✳

"Hmmm," he muttered. "The jungle seems quiet and peaceful tonight."

Wait, who was that? He gave out low growls. His sensitive ears zoned in on activity as they flicked around, searching the dark for any movement.

He had to be careful.

The protection he provided could not be absolute and without restrictions. The free will of these souls must be allowed to reign. Though Mauroga used his power and intervened when needed, this had to be done within limits.

As an Ancient, he had the ability to exercise strong charms. Nevertheless, he remained bound by cosmic laws plus obligation and oath to the overlord, Rath.

"Ah...," he rumbled.

Whiskers twitching, he smelled the scents riding on the night breeze. His ears moving to and fro, he tuned in to the sounds of the late hour.

Tiny creatures hurried in the blackness. Small feet moved nimbly as they scurried in the shadows.

"Grrr!" Mauroga shook his head, picking up a stinky waft.

It was Goom'pa and D'uh.

With resignation, he listened to the approach of two pairs of scampering feet. Where were they off to at this late hour? *Brats.* He frowned. How did they always find a way to keep him on his toes?

Lights from the heavens shone above Palidon. The beams danced on the leaves and forest floor, showering silver rain on the thick, green foliage.

"Groo, groo, groo!" Goom'pa waved puny arms to express urgency. Then he sped off with surprising quickness.

If one listened closely, the speech of the Poofys sounded like mini grunts. Translated for the human ear, this is what the listener would have heard...

"Let's go, D'uh!" Peering over his shoulder, Goom'pa raced on miniscule paws and gathered speed. The Poofys walked upright like playful little humans. However, when in a hurry, they sprinted on all fours.

"Groo, groo! Ya, ya, what fun we'll have!" D'uh chattered with excitement as they flew across the starlit woods, bounding through the gloom of the night hours.

Quick and nimble, Goom'pa showed the way. Focused, he wove a path over rocks, vegetation, roots, and all the other obstructions their slight bodies encountered.

Off they went, to visit the Varleys.

Chief ranger of Miron National Forest, John Varley had held this position for the last twenty years. The man loved his job, and in Emma he had a caring wife. For many a contented season, they'd lived in their comfortable cottage in the forest.

The clock showed nine o'clock in the evening. The couple had settled down to view a favorite TV show after a delicious dinner prepared by Emma. The tattered screen door allowed for the cool night scents to drift into the house.

The Poofys scampered up the low-lying bluffs, over boulders and rocks. Chests heaving from exertion, at last they came to a sudden stop. Perched on top of a boulder, they sighted the cabin in the distance. The cottage glowed, lit up for the evening. The Varleys lounged in contentment in their living room.

Goom'pa's sniffs told him the humans had enjoyed roast chicken and potatoes for dinner. His partner also took in the scents. Both drooled, overwhelmed by the aromas of the recent feast. Little tummies rumbled with hunger; whiskers trembled.

"Slurp, yum." D'uh licked his chops.

From experience, they knew they couldn't go directly to the cottage. Something would make them feel confused and head back home. This happened because of the magic spell cast by the Elanian fairies to protect the small creatures and shield their land. The Poofys remained completely ignorant of this, yet felt the effects.

But Goom'pa, he was quite smart. Well, at least in certain ways.

"Come on, D'uh, let's go." While he wasn't entirely sure what prevented them from moving forward, he'd figured out a way around the force.

"Ohh, yum, yum, me so ready!" squeaked out D'uh. "The munchy meal must have been good!" He rubbed his paws together, warm brown eyes gleaming in the night.

Goom'pa shot forward, approaching right up to where the mysterious energy obstructed them. With a mischievous look, he squinted back, waiting for D'uh to catch up.

As Goom'pa caught his breath, his poof shone under the star beams. The Poofys had distinctive tufts of fur that stood up on their heads. Beneath the starlit sky, D'uh's scruff also glistened. Quite notably, his poof was dented, and thus unique.

Without further pause, Goom'pa bent over and clawed feverishly at the ground. Within seconds he'd dug a deep hole, his feet sticking out. At a rapid pace, he bored a narrow passage under the earth, and his pal followed.

Working swiftly, they pushed forward.

Goom'pa burrowed up and surfaced. Upon peeping out, he confirmed that all looked clear and shook off most of the dirt. Some still clung to his unwashed, oily fur.

"Chooee, chooee!" He made kneeshees—little sneezes. The golden powder, the soil, tickled his delicate nose.

D'uh closed on him. With outstretched paws, Goom'pa reached down and pulled D'uh out. He brushed at sprinkles of dirt all over his friend's dented poof.

Their hard work had scooped out an underground passage of about six inches. The tunnel took them outside the protection circle formed by the Magic Bubble.

Mauroga noted their activities and hissed under his breath. With stealth, he had crept up to the edge of the woods and crouched low behind a clump of bushes. The cat appeared ghostly in the shadows.

"Grrr..." He didn't approve of these adventures, even though the two were exercising their independence.

Full of mischief, they were curious and impossible to predict. He frowned.

"Chooee!" Goom'pa made another kneeshee. The duo scampered the last few hundred yards to the house.

✳ ✳ ✳

With leaps and bounds, they raced up the patio steps, each one almost three times their height.

Carefully, they moved in silence to avoid disturbing Buddy, the muscular, beige Labrador that belonged to the Varleys.

Yes, he was huge.

The pooch lay right next to his master's feet. John reclined on the couch, enjoying TV along with Emma.

The dog's lids drooped, fighting a losing battle. His dinner had been a large meal consisting of leftover roast chicken and other marvelous stuff Emma had mixed up for him. After gorging himself on a big bowl of goodies, he'd licked the bowl clean till it shone. His tummy was swollen tight. The sounds from the TV and the coolness of the evening breeze blowing in through the open windows enticed him to nap. Finally, he gave in and began to breathe heavily. With his face squished between his large front paws, he was passed out on the wooden floor.

With urgency, the Poofys scurried along the side of the house. Upon spotting the living room window ajar, they bounced high up and onto some potted plants. Without hesitation, they jumped again and landed on the windowsill.

The backs of John and Emma's heads were visible as the couple relaxed and enjoyed a show. Goom'pa's sensitive nose alerted him to the Labrador's bulky presence. Beside him, his chum crouched, taking in the scene.

Moving like little ghosts, they dared not risk disturbing the dog. The two leapt lightly through the opening and landed on a wooden chair. Nimbly, they slid down one of its legs and descended to the rug covering the floor. The fibers of the carpet made D'uh itchy, and he screwed up his impish face, performing quick scratchies.

Goom'pa gestured with his miniature arms. "Come on. We have no time to waste!" He regarded D'uh with expressive eyes.

Given that Buddy slept so close by, being on the living room floor for long was dangerous.

A tail stuck out. The couch blocked their sight of Buddy's muscular body.

John sipped iced tea, enjoying the action-packed TV drama. In silence, the Poofys tiptoed toward the kitchen.

Ah, there it was, the Amazing Yellow Box! That was their understanding of the trash can. Neither had any idea what garbage might be.

"Groo!" Grins of delight broke out on their faces, since they knew the box contained many yummy-smelling (stinky to the human nose) treasures. Eagerly, they bounded up to it and clambered in with haste.

Yes, plenty of goodies to be had!

Without further hesitation, they pounced on the feast. Delicious chicken bones with lots of succulent meat left on them made a banquet for the Poofys. No less tasty were the potato skins and other quite exotic leftovers. A bounty to be had, for sure; enough remained to feed two dozen of their kind.

Hungry, the friends dug into the remnants of the greasy dinner with their sharp teeth. In minutes, they'd gorged themselves on the tasty delights. Their shiny coats glistened with grease and oils from scrambling in the garbage.

Wiping his whiskers clean, D'uh climbed back up and looked around. Nobody had taken any notice. Without pause, he swung from the ledge of the can and landed heavily on the yellow-tiled kitchen floor. Coming down right beside, Goom'pa hit the ground with a thud.

Both collapsed, bellies swollen. With delicate pink tongues, they licked themselves clean. Now that had been a real treat!

"Burppp!" Goom'pa covered his whiskers with both paws, pupils wide with alarm.

"Groo, be careful!" D'uh gave Goom'pa an anxious look.

Half-asleep, the pooch in the next room flicked his left ear and struggled to open his drooping eyelids. Had he sensed something? Upon hearing nothing further, he gave in to the drowsiness.

After resting a bit, Goom'pa and D'uh stood up and headed back to the living room.

The Varleys continued to relax ever more. The sounds from the TV soothed the couple. The uninvited guests monitored the big dog's heavy breathing.

The Poofys leapt back up to the windowsill and were soon seated cross-legged, near the right corner to avoid being spotted. It would have taken a keen eye to detect their presence as they squatted less than a couple inches high.

The two settled down for a favorite after-dinner treat, watching TV! They had gone through this routine for years.

In wonder, they took in the sights and sounds that flowed from the lit-up screen.

However, they lacked understanding of what made the gadget work. D'uh pondered how a truck or a train got inside the box! However did so many people live in it? But they didn't question the TV too much. It must be magic, and that was that.

Over the years, they'd learned a never-ending variety of things from viewing various programs.

✳ ✳ ✳

The Varleys remained unsuspecting of the Poofys' presence. On such occasions, Buddy thought he picked up a stinky whiff. But over time, he came to ignore the aroma as just another one of those forest scents invading the house.

Tonight, husband and wife checked out a popular hospital serial.

Goom'pa and D'uh quickly caught on to the main details of the plot. They studied the patient. He lay on the bed while the doctor took care of him.

Poofys were extremely keen and imitated numerous things they saw on TV. They brought the lessons with them to the environs of their magical realm. They even had a Small Animal Hospital (SAH), run by Sadsak (Small Animal Doctor, Small Animal Kingdom).

Tonight, the teeny, well-fed critters sat perched atop the windowsill. Full of curiosity, they eagerly watched the story unfold, their bellies plump with yum.

The hour was peaceful.

Crouched in his hideout, Mauroga squinted from behind the foliage, alert. Silence reigned over the dark. It was a quiet evening.

And then, the night exploded into chaos!

D'uh began to nod off from the effects of the rich meal. The dented poof drooped as his head lolled at an angle while he fought the drowsies. His furry tuft shone dully in the glare of the TV. Colorful images flashed across the screen.

In slow motion, he keeled toward his partner. As he tilted, one of his whiskers tickled Goom'pa's nose.

"Chooee!" Goom'pa sneezed—too minor a sound to be made out by humans, but Buddy's sharp ears instantly picked it up.

What was that? Startled, the dog came fully awake. "WOOF!! WOOF!!"

"Hush!" chided Emma.

"Quiet!" said John. The plot required concentration.

The pooch jumped up with alarming quickness. His sudden movement caused D'uh to yelp. Surprised, he fell backward and off the windowsill, onto the patio. Goom'pa followed in haste.

The Labrador's powerful muscles tensed. He'd heard the sneeze! On full alert, his agile body launched into a sprint and shot out of the room.

"Groo! Go, go, go!" Goom'pa called out to D'uh, trying to rouse him out of his fright.

The two wouldn't even make for a meager munchy treat were the Lab's massive jaws to seize on them.

Both Poofys scuttled, scampering quickly away from the porch. Buddy skidded around the corner and took off like a bullet. The Lab's pace quickened as he pursued the faintly visible, minute creatures. His prey scurried in haste toward the jungle darkness and away from the cottage lights.

As a result of the lavish meal he'd eaten, D'uh moved a tad sluggishly. Still groggy, he tried to shake off the sleepy buzz in his head.

"Groo!" urged Goom'pa. At this pace, they wouldn't make it to the tunnel!

The big dog ate up the distance with long strides. It was quite impressive, though, how swiftly the two dots moved.

But the Lab was closing in.

With a powerful lunge and a snap of his huge jaws, he almost made a meal of D'uh!

Mauroga tensed as the dog approached the terrified Poofys. With azure eyes, he gauged the situation.

Rising up, he bared his fangs. All senses on high alert, he emerged speedily from his nook.

Three times Buddy's height, he could have thrown the pooch a hundred yards with one flick of his mighty paw. Nevertheless, he paid heed to a greater law and avoided leaving Palidon unless he had no other choice.

"GRRRROOWWWWW!" A menacing snarl came from Mauroga, the rumble sending chills down the spines of all creatures nearby.

Yes, Buddy heard the ominous warning, which made his fur stand on end.

In response, he braked hard. His paws skidded, throwing up dirt. Suddenly very scared, he backed away.

Who was out there? Confused, the dog slunk off. With a last look, he scooted home. What had he heard? The night was much too dark to detect anything.

The two Poofys used the dog's hesitation and quickly dove down the tiny passage they had dug up earlier.

Meanwhile, Buddy bounded back in haste to the comfort of the living room. There, the pooch settled down, heart pounding. That sound! The big dog still trembled. The memory put a chill in his bones.

✳ ✳ ✳

The Poofys emerged from the tunnel into Palidon, runty bodies covered with the golden powder.

"Chooee! Chooee!" The two had the kneeshees from the dirt thrown up by their daring activities.

The friends shook off the grime as well as they could and exchanged meaningful looks. With all that excitement, their hearts were still racing.

Then, without warning, they broke into mischievous smiles and clapped one another on the shoulder.

"Groo! Ha, that was close!" Goom'pa grinned at D'uh.

Little rascals. Mauroga ground his teeth. He wished he could grab their scruffy, puny necks! He wanted to roar at them! How dare they put him through so much worry on their account?

The Poofys danced their way home under the starlit sky that covered the enchanted forest. The big cat quietly climbed high into the jacaranda tree and settled in for the nightly vigil.

Peace reigned in the Poofy kingdom once more.

At least for now...

✳ ✳ ✳

7

GOOM'PA GETS A BONKY!

Sun smiled bright on Palidon, raining yellow gold on the abundant green covering the enchanted land. Blissful, he shined happily on its inhabitants.

The willows, mighty oaks, jacarandas, pines, and banyans entwined in harmony, producing a thick and protective canopy. Hundreds of different types of plants and shrubs joined forces, creating a second layer of cover and protection for Palidon's residents. The foliage also provided food—nuts, berries, and honey created from a dazzling variety of matchless flowers. The forest nourished myriad creatures dwelling in the mystical realm.

The animals scurried about on their daily activities, the big and small, the slow and fast ones.

The blossoms swayed in the early morning breeze.

The birds of Palidon piped a joyful song of beauty and hope and their delight in simple pleasures. Mamas fluttered along, busy as they went about the task of gathering munchies. The babies waited, hungry, in the nests.

Papas built and strengthened the homes, nestled in branches of strong trees. Thus, they made sure the young ones lived protected and in warmth. Back and forth they flew with twigs and leaves in their beaks. These were used to build and bolster the nests.

✳ ✳ ✳

Early each day, the Poofys awoke and popped their heads out of their cave-holes. With dreamy gazes, they blinked open their eyes. The creatures yawned, showing tiny, sharp teeth, and out-stretched their slight arms.

A keen observer would have sighted the poofs rising out of the underbrush as sleepy faces emerged to greet the day.

For safety, they built homes underground by digging up the soil. For further security, they dug out underground caves beneath thickets and dense shrubs, hidden from passersby. The narrow entrance of these dens prevented the bigger forest animals from reaching in with their paws. Though the larger snakes might try and slide in, the smaller ones knew far better. If someone got curious, Poofys could give bits and bities that stung.

Morning had broken over Palidon. Goom'pa stirred in his home deep under the earth. Whiskers twitched as he opened his eyes and sensed daylight filling the entrance with a dim glow. The rising sun called.

First, he scanned for signs of intruders or lurking danger. All appeared calm, and he clambered out of his domain.

Upon standing up, Goom'pa stretched and grunted; his little body hungry and thirsty. Lickety-split, he climbed up a bush. The moisture sat plump on the leaves, not yet touched by the daylight warmth to come.

The Poofy reached out with a delicate paw as he straddled a branch. He gave a gentle tug to a dew-laden leaf. With his teeny, pink tongue, he drew in the fat and wobbly gloop drop.

"Gulp...groo!" Goom'pa seemed cockeyed for a second. He focused on the drop as it disappeared into his mouth.

"Mmm...groo...groo." The water tasted clean and nourished his body.

Light on his feet, he jumped from one hedge to another. Ahh, his favorite, a blueberry bush!

Tummy rumbling, he peered close at a juicy berry. It reflected clear in his hopeful eyes, and he broke into a grin of delight. The prize hung heavy from the branch with ripeness. The Poofy clambered onto a strong limb, gripping it with both legs. With eager front paws, he plucked off the fruit.

Oh! The treat felt weighty.

Losing his balance, Goom'pa fell onto the grass carpet. For a moment, he rested on his side, clutching the sweet ball with elfin hands. The offering was as big as his face.

"Groo!" He feasted on the fruit, letting out smacking sounds. "Groo, grooo, ohh, yum, yum!"

With gusto, he ate the whole munchy and burped. Sticky juices covered his fur. Brown eyes shining with contentment, Goom'pa felt his strength return quickly.

✳ ✳ ✳

"Goom'paaaaa!" Ro-Ro, the Poofy's close friend, called out to him. "Where are you? Come out and play!"

"Right here!" Licking his moustache clean, Goom'pa bolted out from under the blueberry bush.

A plump little Poofy approached, tramping through the underbrush with a lazy motion. The furry form was chubby and round, a lighter brown than the rest of his kind. Noted for his poof, which stood out dark chocolate and pointy, he was known to the others from far away by his shape. A happy fellow, Ro-Ro swayed side to side as he strolled.

"Come, come! There is a real treasure to be had this day." Ro-Ro flashed a big, toothy grin.

"Groo...what have you been up to?" Goom'pa regarded his friend with interest.

Ro-Ro walked as if doing a dance. "What do you know?!"

The plump creature's eyes were wide with excitement. "Extra hungry, I sniffed around the area at daybreak. Lo and behold, I came upon some special goodies that Bomboni the squirrel has stashed away. Come, let me show you." He gestured for his playmate to follow.

Despite Goom'pa having reservations, his curiosity got the better of him. The two hurried off, with Ro-Ro leading. They didn't quite scamper or bound away, for Ro-Ro moved at a leisurely pace.

Soon, they stood under the shade of a massive oak, its thick roots spread in every direction. One root rose up before burying itself into the rich jungle soil. The pair waited under the archway it formed, trying to cool off and catch their breaths.

The fast-rising Sun rapidly warmed the woods.

"Do you see?" Ro-Ro pointed at the canvas of branches and leaves spread high above.

"What are we looking for?" asked Goom'pa.

"On the lighter-colored limb, just where the fork begins. Now can you spot it?" Ro-Ro stood still, tilting his head to show his friend exactly where to look.

Goom'pa gazed up, bunching his brow while scratching himself. The running and sweating made him itchy below the stinky fur.

"Yes, way up on the tree." With sharp eyes, Goom'pa focused in the direction his plump pal pointed.

In the thicket of the dense oak, the Poofy spotted a faint object. There rested a nest of leaves and shoots on a fork in the tree's branches.

"I caught a glimpse of Bomboni scurrying in the early light," Ro-Ro explained. "From the smell of it, he carried a yum munchy. I hid in the brush and watched him run up the trunk. And he went to that nest." Ro-Ro's expressive eyes widened.

"So that's where Bomboni lives!" Goom'pa delicately straightened out his poof. "And then?"

"Well, he climbed down in haste and took off again!"

"Have you ventured up yet?" Goom'pa asked in curiosity.

"Uhh, heh, heh..." Ro-Ro gave a sheepish smile while scratching his belly. "I wanted to share the feast with you!" More so, Goom'pa knew, if his friend could avoid having to work for them. Ready for another round of munchies, Ro-Ro blushed when his stomach rumbled.

Goom'pa knew that, unlike most Poofys, his buddy wasn't very agile. As Ro-Ro readied for the climb, he hesitated, bracing his well-fed figure against the tree.

"Groo...OK, let's do this!" Swiftly, Goom'pa scaled up. Since this Poofy was quite nimble of body, his sure grip on the rough-textured bark made getting up to Bomboni's den a piece of cake. However, Goom'pa didn't race, but paused often to reach down and give his partner a helping paw.

With great effort and enthusiasm, Ro-Ro followed, breathing hard as he tried to keep up.

The two reached the fork in the branches. The nest was now within sight. Bomboni's home rested high in the oak. Here, under the cover of the thick leaves, the air was still quite refreshing. However, the two Poofys were hot from their physical efforts.

Full of excitement, they scooted up to the den and peered in.

Why, here was a treasure trove! They spotted dozens of peanuts stashed away. Most of the peanuts were huge, the shells as large as their bodies or larger.

"The smell! Ahh, yummy. But where is Bomboni getting his stash from?" Ro-Ro's eyes widened as he swayed.

"So many of them!" His fellow Poofy, Goom'pa, scratched his head as they gaped in awe.

"Slurrrppp." Ro-Ro could barely contain himself, patting his belly.

Giddy with excitement, they climbed into the nest. Not quite the athlete, Ro-Ro kind of tumbled in.

Fast, Goom'pa snatched a peanut and turned to make a hasty escape. He paused to squint back.

"What exactly do you think you're doing?" he asked Ro-Ro.

His greedy associate had grabbed a nut as big as himself. Swaying unsteadily, he tried to clasp it with both arms.

"Groo! Seriously, you are one crazy Poofy, Ro-Ro! How will you climb down with that giant peanut?" On the alert, Goom'pa glanced about to check if their presence had been noted.

Silent, Goom'pa's partner gave him a mysterious smile. Without a word, he tipped the prize over the ledge.

The two followed the falling peanut with sharp eyes, their poofs and whiskers peeping out over the rim of the nest. Ro-Ro's prize bounced among the branches and dropped onto the grass carpeting the jungle floor. Although the maneuver had been effective, Goom'pa had misgivings about the excessive noise.

"Hmmm, Ro-Ro, your mind is crafty where munchies are involved!"

Though Goom'pa tried to wrap slender arms around his own loot, it was also too bulky.

"Oh, well." With a shrug of his shoulders, Goom'pa attempted the same trick. The shell clattered as it fell and came to rest on the ground under the umbrella of a budding bush.

"Hiss!" The racket from the falling nuts had attracted attention.

At full sprint, Bomboni stormed into the clearing out of nowhere. Furious, he inspected the stolen booty lying at the base of the tree.

"Grrr!" *The brats.*

He decided to teach the daring little bandits a good lesson. Baring sharp teeth, he glared up at the nest. His watchful eyes had detected the dots climbing down in haste.

"No way! Want to make an escape, do you?" With stunning speed, the squirrel shot straight up the oak. Halfway there, their paths would cross where the trunk grew stocky and wide.

Compared to the Poofys, Bomboni appeared to be a giant. The duo would pay dearly once he nabbed them.

In an effort to shake him off, they scrambled with urgency. But the squirrel charged them, fast as lightning.

He took a swipe with his claws and narrowly missed the two. With a hasty dance, they dodged his clutch. A mad scramble followed around the tree.

How could they possibly flee from the determined squirrel that outpaced them with such ease?

Unless...

Ro-Ro let go of the trunk and lazily dropped to the bottom of the oak.

Desperate, Goom'pa jumped also, as Bomboni's claws were less than an inch from his scruffy neck. As he spun and fell, he bounced off one leaf and landed on another. He leapt hurriedly toward a branch, clasped it, and swung away. Heart pounding, he touched down in the thicket on his paw-feet.

Both Poofys scrambled up, covered with golden powder as a result of the desperate escape. As quick as a wink, they shook themselves off, Goom'pa still groggy from all the bouncing around.

They had no time to waste, as Bomboni had eyeballed their route. Without hesitation, they took off at a full-out sprint. In haste, they seized the loot and scuttled to make their getaway.

Neither realized they were no longer being chased. The squirrel had rushed back to his lair to examine what kind of a mess had been left behind. For now, he'd lost interest and didn't care to follow the thieves.

Not knowing that, the two little criminals hauled their plunder unsteadily and fled. In desperation, they glanced back occasionally, still shook up from their tumble.

Unnerved from the bumpy ride from the high nest, Goom'pa tried to seek safety. Disoriented, he looked every which way to detect any danger. And then, all of a sudden, it was too late!

Whack! He ran hard into the limb of a low-lying shrub, smacking his forehead.

The last thing he remembered was trying to hold on to the peanut. A delicious darkness overcame him.

In a struggle to keep up, Ro-Ro staggered behind Goom'pa, large prize in tow.

Thud! He saw his buddy go down just as they reached the shadows under the cover of a dense, low-lying bush. Setting aside the peanut, Ro-Ro swayed over to his pal.

"Goom'pa! Goom'pa, are you OK?" Anxious, Ro-Ro eyed his friend and kneeled beside his comrade's puny form.

But Goom'pa, pink tongue sticking out to the side, wasn't moving. His body was stretched out stiff and eyes shut tight.

Gently, Ro-Ro rested his friend's head in his lap. He looked down at the still figure and ran a loving paw across the poof.

"Groo...groo! Hey, bud, talk to me. Please wake up!" Ro-Ro's gaze was full of concern. Yet Goom'pa remained quiet.

And then, Ro-Ro stood up and made a distinctive cry, a Poofy call for help.

Sharp and piercing, the signal was meant only for the ears of the select. In times of trouble, the sound carried as a distress beacon sent out to all Poofys.

✳ ✳ ✳

The others had been engaged in various kinds of daily morning chores and activities when the alarm went out. It was heard across all of Palidon. The dozen or so who were nearest, dropped whatever they happened to be doing at the moment. Some had been taking nappies. Up in a blink, they shot out of their cave-holes in the direction of the call for assistance.

A Poofy in danger needed their help.

Upon arrival, they would again call out to the rest. The second cry should inform them if added help was needed or the matter had been sorted out.

In different corners of Palidon, the Poofys stood up, their trembling paws held in front, eyes wide with worry.

Plinka and Sadsak, being close by, ran at full tilt.

"Groo...groo!" Now Ro-Ro let out smaller sounds, knowing the others were getting close. With tenderness, he cradled Goom'pa and used squeaks to guide the party to their location.

In a jiffy, their friends arrived on the scene and surrounded them.

"Why Goom'pa be still?" Plinka wrung his little paws.

He too was a close and beloved friend of Goom'pa. Even for a Poofy, Plinka was tiny. He had a thick tuft on his head with a bright silver streak.

"Out of my way, the lot of you!" Sadsak marched up to the patient and knelt down, solemn.

At that moment, all gathered around were genuinely concerned.

"Carry him to the SAH please!" spoke Sadsak, with all the authority of any doctor.

Four pairs of paws quickly lifted Goom'pa and followed the doc. The rest trailed behind. Ro-Ro stayed back for a moment to hide the peanuts, and then jogged to catch up with the procession.

The party headed for the Small Animal Hospital. After a few minutes, they sighted a large bush with bright, shiny flowers under the cover of a weeping willow.

The posse made its way into the depths of the turf under the thick shrub. One could barely detect the entrance to SAH until they separated the blades of grass to expose an opening.

Still unconscious, Goom'pa was carried deep into the tunnel below.

The cave-hole was cool. Tiny slits let in light and air from the outside. Plus, the Poofys' sharp vision could sight well in the faint glow.

The patient was placed on the hospital bed gently, with care.

"Ro-Ro." The doctor turned and glared grimly at the pudgy, sorrowful figure. Fact was Sadsak always had a serious expression, having no other choice. On the show some of the Poofys had watched at the Varleys' residence, the physician was ever so grim, and they all had told Sadsak so.

"Yes!" The chubby one looked down, clearly miserable.

"Fetch me a blueberry. Make haste! Later, I'll want to know what the two of you were up to. Go right away. Your bud has a bonky. Please hurry along."

The plump Poofy nodded his head, avoiding the doctor's stern gaze. Making an ungainly exit, Ro-Ro swayed wildly, knocking down a few Poofys.

"Groo...give me space!" pleaded Sadsak.

Meanwhile, the patient continued to lie still.

The Poofys had learned from TV that hospitals had beds. Thus, Goom'pa was laid on an empty matchbox, taken from the garbage can at the Varleys'. The sheets were bunched, dried leaves.

Sadsak bent his ear to the unconscious form. The elfin being breathed faintly and the bump on his head had grown quite visible. With deliberate strokes, the doctor licked the tender area to calm and clean it. The others looked on, grim.

"Soon, I come back!" Plinka climbed out the entrance and belted out the Poofy cry once more. Thus, the rest were alerted that the crisis was being dealt with. Extra hands were not required right now.

"Let me run a check on him." Sadsak stuck a toothpick into Goom'pa's open mouth. This happened to be another gift from the Amazing Yellow Box. It was the SAH thermometer. The Poofys, including Sadsak, had no idea what it was for. Nevertheless, the medical serials showed the doctor used the item often. Hence, they had done their best to copy the device.

Finally, Sadsak pulled the toothpick out and put it away. Gingerly, he stroked the patient's bonky to cool the bump.

Upon his return, Ro-Ro tumbled heavily through the entrance, holding on tight to a single, large blueberry. He seemed too scared to ask how his buddy fared.

The doctor accepted the fruit with his front paws, regarding Ro-Ro with a serious eye. Ro-Ro looked sheepish. These two had obviously gotten into some kind of mischief, but that story would have to wait.

Turning around, Sadsak walked over to the patient. The lickies on the swelling had calmed it down already. Lightly, Sadsak bit into the fruit and broke the skin. The aroma from the juices made every Poofy in the group slurp and drool.

Still, they were quietly respectful except for some scratching. The healer held the yummy offering close to Goom'pa's whiskers.

No response.

With effort, he pressed a little bit of juice out of the berry and rubbed it over the patient's muzzle. For good measure, he squeezed a drop into his ward's mouth.

Again, no reaction...at first.

Abruptly, the subject's nose twitched, and he made sniffies! His tongue stuck out further and licked up the sweet juice. Opening his eyes, Goom'pa sat straight up, still a bit groggy.

"Groo...groo...grooooo!" Cheers erupted among the group.

Even Sadsak wore a faint smile as he placed the treat on Goom'pa's soft tummy. The eager fellow grasped it and ate with gusto.

"Groo?" He looked at the doctor. "Groo, groo, what happened? Why am I here?" His head felt tender from the bonky.

Ro-Ro awkwardly told the story of their adventure.

"Grrroo!" The others grinned at the tale of mischief, while Sadsak scowled his disapproval.

"Looks good. He is going to be OK." Everyone breathed a sigh of relief.

"Thanks, doc!" Goom'pa looked at the doctor with sincere appreciation.

"You'll do fine. Go now, and behave, you brats!" The physician gestured everyone out.

Ro-Ro hugged his pal.

Goom'pa embraced him back.

Without further delay, they promptly took off on a mission. Delicious peanuts waited to be recovered!

✳ ✳ ✳

8

GOOM'PA HAS A FEELING

The hour was late. Night reigned over Palidon. The dense green foliage had turned blackish blue with the dark. Silver star-beams rained from above. A sliver of crescent moon peeked down at the woods.

Wispy clouds hung motionless high up in the night. Translucent and like cotton, they reflected pink, indigo, and green glows from the bejeweled firmament.

It was bedtime in the little kingdom.

Poofys curled up in their tiny homes, asleep. Some nursed their thumbs, lost in young-animal visions of treats and munchies. One gave out an excited grunt. In his dream he found a giant cherry! Another twitched; tiny limbs pawed the air. The little creature visualized running fancy-free in the fragrant flowering meadows.

Almost all slept in their dens.

But one stirred, fully awake. Sleep wouldn't come. What caused this restlessness, he didn't know.

Around ten o'clock that night, Goom'pa tried going to bed, well fed this day on a berry and a peanut. It had been a busy day in the kingdom, and his wee body was nicely tired.

The Poofy should have been drowsy and quickly fallen into a slumber, as most of them did. Curled up, he breathed gently through his delicate pink nose. His whiskers moved rhythmically as he sucked on a thumb.

However, he couldn't relax.

Opening his eyes, Goom'pa pulled the wet digit out of his mouth and rose up. Careful to avoid banging his poof against the ceiling, he sat in the dark for a while.

What was it that troubled him? Over the past few weeks, his soul had become restless, his heart felt dull, as if a part of it were missing.

In an effort to collect his thoughts, he smoothed out the bed of dry leaves.

Crunchies and munchies, scratchies and nappies, Goom'pa led a simple and sweet life.

"Groo!" He shook his head and scratched his bristles. This wasn't the first time he'd been restive. Of late, he had been having trouble nodding off. The easy, natural slumber he was used to didn't come.

Nope, he saw no point in trying to force sleep tonight.

With one swift motion, he was up and climbed down the three miniature steps from the loft. Wide awake, he crawled across the narrow tunnel to the entrance and prepared to emerge from his lair.

Cautious, he popped his head out of the cave between the roots of the thick shrub shielding his home. In the low light, he squinted, catching glimpses of the night.

Yes, mind made up, he knew what to do.

On swift paw-feet, he jumped out and followed one of the paths. These had been carved by the daily movements of bigger animals as they went about their chores.

Enjoying the quiet, he inhaled deeply, taking in the jungle smells gliding on the cool wind-currents. In silence, he skipped along through the woods. His oily poof shone dully in the dim glow of the after-hours.

Goom'pa picked a path through the vegetation, moving with care. For the better part, he traveled in the shadows to evade attention from the night-dwellers in Palidon.

But even though his form was invisible to most, merging with the underbrush, he had been noticed.

✳ ✳ ✳

Shanista, a great white owl, wise one, sensed someone stirring. Perched on the branch of a tall sequoia tree, she didn't miss anything. This night guardian of the kingdom spied the slightest movement in the gloom with her clear, gray eyes.

"Whoo, whoo, whoo! What beckons you this late, young Poofy? It's your nappy time!"

"Groo...groo. Hush, Great Owl! Though it gives me comfort knowing you keep watch!"

"Whoo...whoo. Are you having trouble dozing lately?" Poofys! Who might fathom what went on in those mischievous minds? She followed his movements, casting a protective eye.

With a light touch, Goom'pa separated the vegetation and waded through the thicket. Upon stopping to catch his breath, he peered up at the cloud cover. A few minutes later, he arrived at his destination, the Meadow of Flowers. This vast area grew lush with thick grasses. A variety of pretty blossoms filled the pasture with bright colors. It was a sight to behold, even at night.

Oaks surrounded the circular field on all sides. Poised at the edge of the clearing, Goom'pa calmed his mind. His soft belly moved gently as he inhaled the fragrance of the evening. With deep breaths, he smelled the rich scent of the blossoms.

The Poofy stayed under the thick leaves of a sea-grape bush. Hundreds of these surrounded the trees that formed a sweeping circle.

Something tugged on his soul. With a start he looked up, inspecting the skies above.

"Groo...such a beautiful eve."

The waning moon cast its beams on Palidon and smiled. The stars shone big and bright, a thousand glorious lights. Drawn to the heavens, Goom'pa climbed a bush's stocky limbs and took it all in with wide-eyed wonderment.

The Universe was singing a song.

Each star struck a distinct tone, a radiant note in a symphony that reached out to those who were able to listen. Shiny sequins, they created pretty patterns and doodles in the deep void of infinity.

Yet, Goom'pa was mindful of more and sensed a presence above the eastern section of the horizon. Searching intently, he focused his sight. Hanging low, there appeared a diamond of a star: flawless, an angelic glow. Its crystalline rays shone directly on him.

For some reason, Goom'pa felt shy. Mesmerized by this glittering light, he pulled himself close to the gap between the leaves and peeped up with one eye. A few whiskers were exposed to its silver rays.

Groo, beautiful jewel. Why did this heavenly light make him feel so restless? Nervous, he had knots in his stomach.

Groo, these feelings? A part of him wanted to reach out for her.

Wait! Who was that? For a second he thought he glimpsed a bluish-green pattern with streaks of white flashing by. But the lights vanished so quickly he wasn't quite sure what to think.

Maybe he had imagined the movement?

Zydaar held his breath and quickly cloaked his form in invisibility. *Careful!* The Ancient chided himself. Be alert! The elfin creature that peeped up from below might have spotted him.

Suddenly, Goom'pa was overwhelmed by a longing he couldn't quite understand. To steady his frame, he clasped on tight to the shrub, whiskers twitching with emotion.

"Gentle one, you are most special!" he heard a voice say in his mind. The radiant star sparkled at him.

"What is thy name?" A shower of silver rays enveloped him.

"I am Goom'pa," he whispered shyly.

"Your presence I can pick up with great clarity. Do you sense mine?"

"Groo, groo...yes, I do."

"I am Shine Star. You must call me Shine."

In awe, Goom'pa gazed up; her reflection shone in his eye. "Shine?"

"Yes, Goom'pa!" she beamed.

"How did you find me?"

"I possess many powers, as Prime Ray's daughter."

Goom'pa continued to peer at the stunning heavenly light, star-struck, not fully understanding the message his mind received, yet knowing its truth.

"Shine?

"What makes my tummy hurt when I look at you? Why do I want to reach for you?"

Definitely the one, she sighed. "It's because we feel the same loving emotions for each other."

"Groo...groo!" He nodded, not quite sure of the words.

Yes, much trouble in the empire was to follow! Zydaar shuddered. The wise angel rolled his pearly white eyes.

Overcome by his response to the princess, Goom'pa was swamped by intense emotions. Head spinning, his grip loosened on the branch. He let go and fell onto the soft grasses. With a small grunt, his body relaxed, and he drifted off into a deep slumber.

Twitchies and snories followed.

"He shall be fine, princess mine." Zydaar zoomed away from Earth faster than a star beam.

A smile played on Shine's lips, as if everything made sense now.

The hours passed. The early sounds and breaking sunlight crept softly into the thicket. Scratching his belly, Goom'pa blinked open his eyes. He got up, poof covered with magic powder.

Groo, had it just been a dream? No! The heart knew.

Hungry and thirsty, Goom'pa scampered over to lick morning dew from a leaf and search for a berry.

Daylight had broken over Palidon.

Far away in the heavens, Shine sparkled and giggled.

✳ ✳ ✳

9

GOOM'PA AND THE SMACKOOS, PART I

Night had descended once more. Safe inside his cave-hole, Goom'pa napped. His tiny frame curled up, eyelids drooped, and he nursed a thumb. His soft, warm belly moved gently with each breath.

His poof was dusty. After a day of play, munchies, and mischief, he rested.

Outside, a cool breeze kissed the leaves. The bright moon waxed, just a tad, above the cloud cover.

Goom'pa surfaced from deep slumber and opened his eyes. Fully awake, he stretched his arms and remembered where he was. He was up in the loft. With dainty paws, he gently brushed his poof and climbed down from the bed of leaves.

The hour had turned late. Shine would be out in the sky like a faultless diamond.

Goom'pa quickly scampered off and away. Playful of mood, he did skippies and headed for the meadows.

Shanista the owl stared in silence from her perch.

Mauroga kept vigil high up in the jacaranda.

The pint-size creature—what was he up to now? The jaguar's massive purplish-black muscles flexed with a muffled disapproval. Mauroga's piercing gaze carefully followed the wee shadow.

The Poofy paused in midstride. The twilight glow in the jungle appeared dimmer than usual.

The heavens had begun to swell with black clouds, not just the wispy type. The moon disappeared behind a large formation, and darkness crowded in.

Making haste, he soon arrived at the Meadow of Flowers.

In anticipation of sighting Shine, Goom'pa gulped hard and his pulse quickened. He felt both shy and eager at the same time. At this hour, she would be a jewel suspended above the eastern horizon.

Goom'pa clambered up a sea-grape bush for a better sighting. Winded from his exertions, he paused to search the sky. "Where you be, Shine?"

The gorgeous, multicolored blooms in the clearing glowed with good cheer on bright, starlit evenings. But tonight, the usually gleaming blades of grasses and the shiny orange, red, pink, and yellow flowers were a grayish blur.

Thick clouds diffused the view beyond.

Disappointment set in; puny shoulders drooped. Filled with loneliness, Goom'pa felt his heart ache for his princess.

What had Shine said they had? He pondered.

"Groo!" He couldn't see his beloved's light, and his chest was full of longing.

"Groo...groo!" He searched, reaching for the clouds with his paws. "Groo, maybe I can move them."

Shine's essence responded to his yearning; she sensed the call. "My joy, Goom'pa! I am here even though you can't see me. The skies are overcast tonight!"

In his awareness, her thoughts rang clear.

"I need your help, Zydaar," she hailed the guardian.

"Princess, all is well?" He flew up to his ward.

"I pine for Goom'pa."

"Dear child..." The angel exuded calming hues and soothing energies. Head bowed, he listened to the plea, frame glistening with light beams.

"Could you please remove the dark formations that obscure the meadow? Goom'pa waits there, searching, trying to find me."

Zydaar studied her. Pristine white radiance emanated from Shine, who shimmered with diamond sparks.

"Young princess, you know thy will is my command. I have the power to move the stormy cover in the blink of an eye," Zydaar answered calmly. "Nevertheless, I implore you not to insist upon that course of action."

The Ancient felt a mixed reaction. Protection and concern stirred as he struggled to fathom what might come of Shine's desires.

"Old friend and guardian, pray tell what troubles your peace? You would turn the heavens upside down to see me happy."

The angel closed his eyes, gathering his ideas. With focus, he extracted stories of the Protection of Palidon from his mind and rolled them into a thought-ball. The ball looked like a crystal globe with moving images playing inside.

Zydaar sent the sphere floating across space, where it disappeared directly into Shine.

Upon receiving the offering, she instantly absorbed everything about the history of Palidon and how it had emerged under special guardianship. Images flashed through her mind with blinding speed.

She saw the encounter between Prime Ray and Rath and heard the condition for free will as reiterated by the Red Giant.

She witnessed the agreement that her father, ruler of the entire manifest world, gave consent to.

Now she understood the guardian's dilemma, his struggle to not disappoint her.

Bowing, she reached out with affectionate and loving rays of light. "You have my gratitude for trusting me with this knowledge. I understand now, more is involved in this decision." Consequences would result from conscious interference with the little kingdom, such as the deliberate act of dissipating the veil of clouds.

"Much is at risk beyond my adoration for Goom'pa." she agreed. "Let the dark eve in Palidon be; may the rainmakers do their dance."

"My love," Shine's voice entered Goom'pa's mind. Her words, to him, were musical chimes.

"Groo!" His bristles trembled.

The love-struck Poofy's eyes searched the skies, soul filled with tender thoughts. Scratching his soft belly, he sought her in the never-ending beyond.

"We may not be able to observe each other tonight. But my heart is with you. You shall hear its song."

Eyes alive with intelligence, Goom'pa received the princess's message. The teeny form had been crouching motionless for more than an hour.

The jungle air had become thick; the storm clouds stood still.

"Groo...groo...! OK, Shine, I come back tomorrow!" Resigned, Goom'pa turned and retreated silently into the underbrush.

In the far distance, Shine radiated devotion.

✳ ✳ ✳

An idea took shape; Goom'pa made skippies down a different path into the late night, headed further away from home. After a while, he entered another clearing.

The vegetation started to climb at this point. The kingdom wasn't hilly, but it did undulate a bit. He approached the highest rise, the Dome.

The woods opened up here. It was a wondrous sight on a clear night.

Groo...tonight is not so. With a sigh, Goom'pa climbed to the uppermost point on the rising ground.

The Dome wasn't much more than a grass-covered knoll, at best a few hundred feet high. Even though he couldn't see her here, each knew of the other's presence.

Standing at the peak of the bluff, Goom'pa was almost invisible in the soft grasses that grew on the hill. From his new vantage point he squinted east, responding to her love.

In his wisdom, Goom'pa clearly knew that this was the closest he could physically approach Shine. Thus, he followed instinct and did what came naturally. Although the Poofy couldn't spot her, he yearned to give her a kissy or two in the best way he knew.

"Chooee!" The grass tickled his moustache as he crouched down. With utmost care, he kissed the golden powder.

Stepping a few feet to his left, he planted another peck on the ground. In deliberate fashion, he repeated the process, yearning to connect with his princess. "Shine will reach down and take them!"

He placed kissies all over the Dome.

The Elanians had woven complex magic to surround and maintain the purity of this land. The innocence of Goom'pa's kissies mixed with the potent spell cast by the fairies. Instantly, the kissies blossomed into plump red balls pulsing with light. The jelly-like round offerings had delicate, shiny, pink buds on top.

Each kissy transformed into a Smackoo...

Without any surprise, Goom'pa eyed his creations, not questioning their beauty. Soon, they covered the whole hill. The squiggly red globes lit up the blackness like glowing lanterns.

The Poofy was finally tired out. His mission fulfilled, making skippies and dancies, he headed home.

Soon he was sucking his thumb, eyes shut tight.

Dreaming of a star, he made grunt-snories.

10

GOOM'PA AND THE SMACKOOS, PART II

The radiance of the Smackoos lit up the clouds and penetrated their thick cover. Shine gazed at the red and pinkish glimmer tinting the skies over the jungle. From her home in the beyond, thousands of millions of miles away, she knew of their presence.

With her abilities, Shine grasped what the Poofy had done. In astonishment, she took it all in. Her heart surged with affection for her Goom'pa. The glowing spheres sent out a strong energy that spanned the far reaches of infinity.

The Elanians at once recognized the event that had transpired. Istara, Head of the Order, most respected of the fairies, was fascinated. In her ancient wisdom, she understood Goom'pa's kisses for the princess were a treasure, to be cherished by the heavens.

Without delay, she convened a council. "The entire reality is greatly affected by the powers of this creature," she told her fellow Elanians. "These gifts must be collected and delivered to Shine Star. It's important this be done right away."

As always, Istara had a plan. It was time to train the young ones, the Glitonian Sparkles, baby angels. Upon becoming conscious of their surroundings, they were put under the charge of Vinorgaan, Master Trainer.

As Istara wove magic twinkles, her thoughts came alive. As she concentrated, they began to twirl and dance around each other, forming wondrous shapes. In a flash, they collapsed into a sleek, silver arrow and shot across the cosmos.

The message entered Vinorgaan's mind, drawing his focus to the urgent matter. Away on a task in a far galaxy, he had been immersed in adjusting the movement of a planet.

Without hesitation, Vinorgaan handed the work over to one of his assistants, Glensarine. "Turn it a half degree to the right. Increase the spin by a bit!" With a deft touch, the angel carried out her master's instructions.

"Glen, you are well trained, almost an expert in matters relating to planets. Shoot me a magic twinkle if you have a concern. I have to leave at once on a matter of much consequence." In haste, Vinorgaan departed, a blazing comet streaking across the heavens.

As he approached Xentar, a gigantic star cluster, Vinorgaan slowed down and sent out the call. Thirty-six Glitonians shot out from various parts of the magnificent formation and surrounded him immediately. Playful baby angels, they emitted many splendid colors. They sparkled and giggled.

The Master Trainer looked on them with affection. "Follow me, young ones! Off we are, on an adventure."

Once again, Vinorgaan shot through the cosmos, eager troop in tow.

Moments later, he knelt before Istara. With infinite patience, he awaited further instructions from the powerful fairy. The Glitonians rotated shyly behind him, having never been in her presence before.

"Do you sense it, Vinorgaan?" Her question rang clear.

"Yes."

A magical event had taken place in the Milky Way. Every sparkle of stardust that made up Vinorgaan's radiant body raced with excitement. Without wasting another moment, Istara brought him up to date on Goom'pa, Shine Star, and the events surrounding Palidon.

"Please take the Glitonians and go forthwith. Complete the work at hand with utmost care and haste."

"Yes, this will be a good training run for the little ones."

Like a starburst, Vinorgaan took off with thirty-six colorful lights in tow. He streaked across the immense stretches of space, slowing down upon his approach to Earth. As he hovered in the green planet's atmosphere, the young ones whirled around him. Playful, they formed a ball of light.

Ever on watch, Mauroga had been resting in the jacaranda tree. In an instant, he changed form and appeared before the new arrivals.

Vinorgaan knelt upon seeing the Purple Angel approach and paid respect.

"Old comrade!" hailed Mauroga's commanding voice. "What draws you to this remote part of the kingdoms? And what's up with these young pups?" He eyed the baby angels watchfully. They gawked, open-mouthed, at this powerful presence.

Without delay, Vinorgaan relayed Istara's directive to him.

Listening with care, the Ancient digested the information. He had sensed mysterious forces at play in Palidon during those late hours.

"I must admit my astonishment," responded Mauroga. By virtue of being an Ancient, he exercised far-reaching authority and didn't deem the matter required Rath's personal attention.

He penetrated Vinorgaan's thoughts. Yes, he sensed clarity and honor.

"Certainly, please go ahead, respected Trainer of Angels. But might I remind you; the creatures of this world must never set eyes on you?"

The Master Trainer bowed his thanks and led his troops to the center of the Dome.

In the blink of an eye, Mauroga sprang back up on the jacaranda. The mighty jaguar rested on a high limb, keeping his attention on the new arrivals.

Vinorgaan and his eager team penetrated the bubble and landed on the hillock. The Elanian spell affected them instantly.

The protection magic turned the Glitonian Sparkles into pint-size elves with green suits, red booties, and golden bells on their hats. They also had one more notable feature. On their backs were transparent silvery wings that allowed them to hover in midair.

"Attention!" The trainer kept his voice low as his feet touched down on the gentle slope. The eager baby elves lined up in front of him. There followed much excitement and whispering.

About a foot tall, sporting warm eyes and a thick brown mustache, Vinorgaan was larger in form than his elves. The small ones stood six inches, with toothy smiles.

"Young Glitonians!" he reached into their thoughts. "Hear me with care, my students. Your mission is of utmost importance, and Istara waits for us to report back."

The elves quieted down, listening in earnest.

"Do you see the how they glow, the globes around you?"

"Yes!" The baby angels nodded. The teeny bells on their hats sparkled and jingled.

The Dome was lit with the lustrous red and pink warmth from the pulsing Smackoos. The shiny spheres were about three inches big and shone like lanterns with lights inside. Aglow, they sat plump and soft.

A curious Glitonian strolled over to the nearest one and poked it with his finger.

"Choo!" The Smackoo jiggled. The elf jumped back, startled and questioning.

"That's correct. They sound like kisses because they are! Now, everybody, collect one and bring them to me. Dawn approaches, we must be quick. No creature of the forest should ever sight us. Let's go."

The elves scurried about their task, picking up the many globes. Silken smooth, each had to be clasped firmly to the chest. When poked or squeezed, they made kissy sounds.

"Choo, choo!"

The youngest, Moof, tripped on his way back to Vinorgaan. In slow motion, he began to roll down the slope. Though wide-eyed and scared, he held on tightly to his Smackoo!

"Choo, choo, choo, choo," it said, as Moof bounced lightly down the gentle slope.

His trainer rushed swiftly to his side. With great gentleness, Vinorgaan picked the young one up. Upon cleaning the dirt off the baby angel's nose, he gave him a peck on the cheek. "Good job, Moof."

The little elf reddened. He was so happy!

The Glitonians lined up on the double. Vinorgaan then cast a spell. Lickety-split they shot away into the night. In an instant, the group was gone.

A keen observer might have glimpsed a shooting star followed by a string of tiny, radiant, colorful lights.

As they left Palidon the babies changed from elves back to their natural form.

The mesa returned to dark again, shrouded under the cloud ceiling. The Smackoos had all been carefully collected. Mauroga regarded the disappearing lights with an open, azure eye. His large paws dangled lazily off the limb he rested on.

✳ ✳ ✳

Soon, Vinorgaan and his young helpers circled Istara once again. From a distance it appeared as if red balls of warmth surrounded her. The Glitonians hugged the glowing Smackoos, oh so proud!

While Vinorgaan was receiving new instructions, Zydaar arrived and joined the group. Under his direction, they shot off and away.

Shine saw streaks of red approach as the party swept in. Her guardian and the trainer were followed by glowing lights. A Smackoo was held by each proud baby angel, gleaming with delight.

The princess had played skippies with them before and recognized the troop. In a playful mood, the Sparkles had wide grins.

She knew that very instant what had occurred. As Zydaar watched fondly, her face lit up with awe.

The Smackoos sailed up to her and were absorbed into her radiant body.

"Choo, choo, choo!" One by one, she received them. With every kiss, she blushed and laughed, pulsing lights of joy.

Amid much merriment and giggles, Vinorgaan and the baby angels were gone.

All had been made right with the universe again.

In Palidon, during the quietest of hours just before the break of dawn, stillness reigned.

Goom'pa slept curled up in his loft. He gave out small snores, lost in dreams of precious Shine.

Light would break soon...

11

GOOM'PA AND THE
GOLDEN TREASURE

"Groo, hurry up!"

"Groo, hold on D'uh, almost done!"

Paw-feet stuck out as Goom'pa dug deep inside the toolbox. The rustlings could be heard faintly by his fellow Poofy.

The duo was back at the Varley cottage.

The clock struck eleven in the late morning. Chief ranger of Miron National Forest, John had left early for work in his SUV.

Earlier, at daybreak, Goom'pa gathered up D'uh.

"Groo, groo!" He had scurried over to his friend's den and beckoned.

Light crept through the thick foliage overlying the land.

That fateful morn, Goom'pa's buddy had been out searching for breakfast. In the midst of eating a ripe cherry, he squatted nearby.

Upon hearing the call, D'uh quickly finished off the feast and scampered over.

"Groo, what's up?" Face covered with sticky juice, D'uh smacked his whiskers and licked off traces of the breakfast.

As he gazed at his associate, Goom'pa appeared solemn, struggling to reach a decision.

Yes, he decided to share the dilemma with his close friend. Thus, he opened up to his playful pal, he of the dented poof.

"Groo, there is something you should know." With serious brown eyes, Goom'pa addressed his confidante.

In response, D'uh stared back, uncertain of what exactly might follow. Patches of magic powder sprinkled his scruff, and remnants of cherry stuck to his pink nose. Goom'pa's solemn face caused him to make scratchies. To ease the gravity of the moment, he somersaulted.

"Groo, listen up, this is important!" the other chided him.

D'uh faced Goom'pa, attempting to concentrate. He shifted around on his paw-feet. Finally, the teeny Poofy settled down cross-legged and squinted.

"I have love feeling for Shine!" Goom'pa announced. "The princess tells me she has kissy for me too. Well, she kind of said that." A dreamy, faraway expression crossed his face while the creature fussed nervously with his poof.

Attempting to control an itch, his puny audience tried to grasp the idea.

Goom'pa explained the plan to get a gift for his darling star.

Not questioning the cosmic makeup of the relationship, D'uh gave a small nod in response. He didn't doubt the bond or, for that matter, the logistics involved. In his world, everything seemed possible, even normal.

"What kind of present?"

"Groo, a fancy one!"

Thus here they were, returning to the ranger's cottage. Where else did you have access to countless wondrous treasures?

By now, the pair had the routine down. The old underpass had held up, and the duo snuck through the opening.

✳ ✳ ✳

With John away, Emma hovered over the stove, preparing hearty dishes for the evening. The aromas from the cooking range and oven made the Poofys' soft tummies rumble and groan. However, they tried to focus on their mission.

Buddy snored noisily, enjoying his post breakfast nap in the living room. In silence, Goom'pa and D'uh scuttled by him and shot across to the kitchen.

Steam rose from the pots and pans bubbling over. The smells of Emma's baking wafted from the oven. With care, she inspected the recipes, wiping her hands on the apron. All the while she remained blissfully ignorant of the two tiny creatures scooting over the yellow tiles toward the garage.

An inch or so gap between the floor and the door led the Poofys to their destination. Silent and fast, they eased through the slit. *Careful. Wouldn't want to bang your poof against the narrow opening.* D'uh's tuft already had a dent, and he felt self-conscious about his crowning glory.

After a quick survey of the parking area, Goom'pa zeroed in upon a sleek red case. The object rested high on one of the metallic rack-shelves lining both sides of the empty car stall.

"Groo, groo!"

"Groooooo!" D'uh had also spotted it.

"That chest looks interesting. While I take a peek, D'uh, you keep an eye on things. Check the weather outside if you can."

The sky had turned increasingly cloudy on the trip over to the Varleys'. The stormy formations pointed to a gloop-fall headed in their direction.

Determined, Goom'pa scampered up to the box on the third shelf.

Meanwhile his partner hurried to the parking entrance. John had closed it when he drove out.

As D'uh checked the lower edge of the garage door, he noted the shutter base had a kink. This created a small opening, but plenty big for them to squeeze through.

"Groo, groo, take a peek at what I found. Look, a new way to get in and out of the cottage!"

Goom'pa had climbed half inside the bin. John kept tools in there. The box hadn't been locked and the lid happened to be loose enough to pry open.

"See, a gap at the bottom of the door. Let me squeeze out for a quick peek."

"Groo, good idea, you go ahead." The objects in the case fascinated Goom'pa. Astonished, he tried to make sense of the riches he'd discovered. Nuts, bolts, spanners, all kinds of fascinating stuff.

There were transparent slits at the top of the door and in the roof. This allowed enough illumination for the Poofys to go about their business.

Plus, they had no clue there existed a light switch. Nor would they have dared touch it. The two had sharp eyes and sighted quite clearly in the minimal lighting.

D'uh slid out under the crack at the base of the parking closure. As he emerged on the driveway, the air crackled with static from a bolt of lightning. With a delicate nose, he sniffed the breeze. The winds were laden with smells of a rapidly approaching thunderstorm. Concerned, he retreated back inside.

"Please hurry, Goom'pa!"

"Give me a second, I'm almost done."

"A heavy storm approaches. I doubt we could journey home without gloop touching us!"

The Poofys were terrified of water. Fact was, the two had never had a bath in their lives. Natural oils protected their fur and bodies. The only regular contact with moisture occurred from the dew they drank or the berries and various fruits they loved to nibble on. Yet that was different from being drenched in a full-fledged rainfall!

"OK, coming..."

The smaller one took stock of the situation nervously while the other Poofy's feet poked out of the red case.

"Ah, look what we have here!" Upside down, Goom'pa reached deep into the toolbox.

"A Golden Cone! This shall make a fine gift for Shine Star." He had spotted a screw. The prize had a dull bronze sheen, though slight rust had set in. Fancy grooves spiraled around its length and the color fascinated him. The find was about an inch long.

"This fine present will surely impress the princess!" Never had he laid eyes on anything like this amazing object. In awe, he pulled it out of the bin. He tried not to scrape his poof as he eased out.

"Let's go!" cried D'uh.

"Yes, yes. I've found what I was searching for."

The object wasn't easy to carry. It was almost half his size and quite bulky for Goom'pa's tiny limbs. He clutched it close to his chest with one arm. Quickly, but with care, he climbed down the shelf using his other paw and nimble claw-feet.

Full of curiosity, D'uh scampered up to look at the find.

Emma continued to buzz around the kitchen, stirring up delicious creations. Buddy slept, unaware of the daring intruders. Well-fed, his senses were dulled by the cooking scents and the rumble of the approaching storm.

In a hurry, the little thieves slid out under the garage exit and dragged the find after them. Each grasped one end of the treasure and the young friends scurried off at full tilt. The tunnel would allow entry to Palidon and get them past the barrier formed by the Magic Protection Bubble.

As fast as they could, the two shot toward the opening of the shaft. They knew it was a few hundred yards ahead. Weighed down by the screw, they pushed forward with an unsteady gait. Suddenly a clap of thunder hit their delicate ears, and the first plump drops came crashing down around them.

The rain smacked the earth, throwing up a smattering of magic powder upon impact. With skill, the duo dodged their way through the falling gloop.

In this race to the finish, thunder and lightning intensified. The rain had transformed into a full-fledged downpour.

Headfirst, Goom'pa dove into the opening and hurriedly pulled the Golden Cone inside. The effort caused him to make little grunts.

Frantic, D'uh helped push the screw into the tunnel and scrambled in behind it. As his paw-feet disappeared into the tunnel, crashing rain pelted the ground where he had been standing just a moment prior. There followed a resounding boom and lightning cracked open the heavens themselves.

Hiding in the passage, the two trembled at the fury of the raging storm. The exertion had made them sweaty under their stinky fur. Both held the trophy tight with soiled paws.

Once their breathing settled, D'uh peeped out the other end of the burrow toward Palidon. His nerves weren't soothed watching the heavy gloop-fall.

"Groo, groo!" He gave out anxious cries. Puddles were forming all over quickly. At this rate, the shallow crawlspace wouldn't offer them protection for very long.

"Groo, groo, groo!" D'uh bleated again, afraid, his whole body trembling.

High in the cover of the jacaranda, Mauroga stirred. Over the sound of crashing thunder, he zoned in on the cries. His little Poofys! Emotions surged as the jaguar's sensitive hearing picked up D'uh's plaintive yelps.

One or more of the tiny ones were in trouble. The big cat flicked his ears in all directions.

"Groo, groo, grooo!" The bleats were barely audible over the storm.

Grrr, those sounds were from D'uh! Mauroga realized exactly where the cries came from.

Moving like greased lightning, he dropped down from the tree. His lithe frame landed lightly on the ground, avoiding splashing in the gloop circles. The rain was coming in sheets and forming pools quickly.

Muscles bunched, Mauroga let out a muffled growl and took off like a bullet. The Poofys' protector headed for the distress call.

Dodging his way through the shower, he sped toward the opening to the crawlspace. Soon he spotted D'uh's dented tuft sticking out. The wee creature trembled.

Curious, Goom'pa joined his friend and also stuck his scrawny neck out to gauge the severity of the situation. Both watched Mauroga's approach, his immense power and swiftness. To see the jaguar during daylight hours was highly unusual.

They caught the determination in his look, and he was soon upon them.

Mauroga extended a massive paw. With the screw in tow, the Poofys clambered on in great haste.

"Rowrr, huh?" The Ancient inspected the object they'd brought along.

Whoever could fathom what these two were up to in their busy lives?

Wasting no time, Mauroga deposited them on his back. The two eased forward and straddled his neck. D'uh bunched up behind Goom'pa with the Golden Cone packed snug between them. The Poofys clung on firmly to Mauroga's purple-black coat. The fur was damp from the moisture.

Mauroga raised his majestic face to the storm above and rumbled in low tones, "Rrrrrr...rrrrrr!" The spell was cast.

The rain didn't touch them any longer. The gloop was blocked by a barrier surrounding Mauroga about two inches from his frame. The droplets splashed down, striking the shield, but didn't penetrate.

D'uh gaped as a huge drop headed directly toward him. It was going to splash his body and wash him away! But at the last second, the rain hit the invisible cloak and splattered into a million dots. It had been only an inch from D'uh's nose. Cockeyed with terror, he'd watched the missile approach his whiskers. Then, in the next second, it was gone.

The cat turned and bounded back into the dense woods. His work done, he couldn't risk being spotted by a human. That would create much disturbance and trouble.

Bulging muscles pulsed with energy as he sped down the path of the mystical jungle.

The two passengers checked out the extraordinary view from the back of Mauroga's thick neck. The ground raced by, a blur of shadows and light. The drops shattered and dissipated right in front of their furry faces.

The gloop-fall became gentler as they traveled deeper into Palidon.

Mauroga slowed down and then came to a halt. He crouched under the branches of the sea-grape bush that covered Goom'pa's home.

"Go now, you busy little things!" he growled at them.

In haste, they slid off his neck, along with their treasure.

"Groo, groo...you are the best, Mauroga. Thank you!"

And just like that, the jaguar disappeared, leaving no sign of his presence behind.

In a hurry, the friends dragged the find inside the protection of the cave-hole. Standing back, they admired the find.

"Groo!" D'uh stared at the screw.

"Grooooo, this shall be a fine offering for Shine. I couldn't have done it, but for your help!"

"Groo." D'uh's brown eyes searched his pal's face; he patted his belly.

Goom'pa understood. Crouching down and reaching into a corner where he stored munchies, he pulled out two sunflower seeds.

In silence, the friends sat down cross-legged and nibbled on the nutritious treats.

They'd certainly had...a most fruitful day.

✳ ✳ ✳

12

SHINE—THE CONFESSION

"Wheeeeee!" Playfully, the Glitonian Sparkles spun around the princess, weaving light webs of orange, aqua, and gold.

As Prime Ray's daughter, she had everything. Yet, she had nothing.

Surrounded by admirers and friends, Shine responded politely.

In a contemplative mood, her vision turned within. But the answer was on her lips.

Goom'pa! Ever since she'd set eyes on him, she breathed love for the little Poofy. Without him, her heart knew loneliness, her soul turmoil.

The gifts of an eternal home meant nothing to the daughter of the heavens anymore. The boon to live life everlasting apart from the one you desired so completely was no less than a curse.

"NO!" Unable to contain her anguish, she cried out.

The play stopped. All of creation seemed to stand still. The whole manifest universe shuddered.

The party in the celestial kingdoms faltered.

"Dear friends, I'm fine! Please be at ease. I had a passing thought. All is OK now." Quickly, Shine composed herself and smiled, offering reassurance to the guests.

She emanated warmth once more. Radiant sparks emanated from her to reassure the loving spirits, the myriad angels surrounding her.

Yet, her playmates were confused. The Glitonians circled Shine uncertainly.

Meanwhile, many billions of miles away, Prime Ray furrowed his brow in concentration. Mind focused, he channeled his immense will to shape a star cluster in the process of forming. Along with an extensive army of masterful and magical helpers, Prime Ray concentrated on birthing the baby galaxy.

This new formation, Celdana, would be a matchless entity. A complex design, it was woven of countless suns, planets, moons, comets, and other energies.

Such work took millions of creative years. Prime Ray checked in once in a while to ensure the intricate process was going smoothly.

"Wait!" Far away, he noted a disturbance in the kingdoms. He sensed Shine's hurt.

"Old spirit." The king looked at Lirotus.

The Ancient had charge of the Sinurian Order of Angels. Charged with the physical maintenance of the universe, they reported directly to Prime Ray and carried out his more profound directives.

"Sire." In physical form, Lirotus was a giant, even bigger than Jupiter.

Distracted, Prime handed over the task to his aide.

"Sweet child!" The emperor shifted focus, reaching out to Shine. "Princess, I sense distress. What troubles you, my love?"

"Daddy!" Respecting the power of his mind, she wouldn't pretend. "Father, despite the wonderful gifts and blessings you shower me with...in spite of the generous offerings dear friends bestow upon me each day...regardless of the fact that the cosmos is my vast playground," Shine sighed. "There is one I cherish in a way I never imagined possible. And now that I know this longing..." She paused.

Heart swirling with concern and unease, Prime listened. "Speak, Shine. Complete your thought. Tell me whom you pine for. Why would this fondness cause so much hurt to my baby?"

She calmed herself, searching her heart, her memories. With focus, she formed a thought-ball. The ball glowed as she extended hands of light and delivered the shimmering globe of a thousand moving images to Zydaar. The Ancient knelt to accept it. He fathomed what was required of him and zoomed away.

Upon arriving at his destination, Zydaar braked to a swift stop and folded his intricately patterned wings. Megalon, Orange Angel, loyal aide to Prime Ray, acknowledged his entrance and accepted the thought-ball for his master. Handover completed, Zydaar flew off.

In haste, Megalon sped to his lord and glided the sphere across to Prime Ray.

The king took a deep breath as the silver circle entered his light. The thoughts, the pictures unfolded like a movie. Yet they were much more real.

He viewed and experienced everything as Shine Star had—all her feelings, including the restlessness and longing, the search, Zydaar's flight to Earth...and the discovery of Goom'pa! He came to know Shine's feelings the first time she had looked upon Goom'pa and thus understood the love they shared.

In vivid detail, Prime Ray journeyed through Shine's heartache, joy, and dilemma: to live an eternity without the one you long for.

Ironic! Who would have imagined being an immortal might be a disadvantage? The king mused.

He didn't question the love between his daughter and this unusual creature. By taking in the thought-ball, he accepted her story as his own. He couldn't allow his offspring to be unfulfilled or in agony.

Prime Ray remembered the moment when he was made aware of his function. The honor and privilege to protect the goodness of the kingdoms was his.

As if it were yesterday, he recalled the discovery of Palidon.

Hmm, strange were the ways of the intelligence at play here! He shook his head, trying to sort through all he now knew.

There is no coincidence, he mused.

The protection of Palidon...

The birth of Shine Star...

Goom'pa and Shine's devotion to each other...

"Istara." In need of direction, his mind searched the cosmos.

"Yes, my king." She responded to the summons.

"Convene the Elanian Council."

"It is done as you speak."

"Thank you, great fairy."

Not wasting a moment, Istara was instantly in touch with the other members of the circle.

Sensing Prime's distress, she flew on wings of lightning. The whole group raced through the kingdoms. Upon arrival before the burdened ruler, the wise beings circled him.

"My lord, what causes such turmoil?"

The king floated a thought-ball to her. It immediately replicated into several identical spheres. All sailed into the powerful minds of the gathered fairies. Thus, they came to know Prime Ray's conundrum, a parent's dilemma.

Of course, they were already intimately familiar with the story of Shine and Goom'pa. Invited when Palidon required protection, the guild had sung a charm to form the Magic Protection Bubble. Their minds were also closely in touch with all that affected the Poofys.

"Help me. My child is in pain."

With concern, they heard a father's plea.

The Elanians' wings slowed down their beat. Joining hands, members of the council merged into a ball of blinding white light. Emitting intense explosions of energy, they united as one mind. Their collective wisdom explored numerous possible solutions to the king's plight, and the universe's dilemma.

Among the endless choices offered, what did the Infinite desire most? How would love unfold on its quest through time?

Yes, the simplest choice remained the wisest. The Elanians separated.

"Prime." Istara had newfound clarity and understanding. "Magic offers endless solutions that may seem to satisfy immediate needs. However, for Shine to be truly happy, the answer should also increase the harmony of the cosmos."

"Advise me, oh thoughtful spirits, what be your insight?" Head lowered in thought, Prime Ray sat on the Throne of Crystals, listening intently.

And so, Istara told him. The final decision was his. The fairies said a prayer.

Time passed. A tear escaped his eye.

"Wise ones, most grateful am I for your sage wisdom. My spirit humbled, I have work to do." He nodded.

The Elanians sang their appreciation, fluttering starlit wings. Then, in the blink of an eye, they were gone.

Mind made up, Prime Ray understood what came next.

✳ ✳ ✳

13

SAVED BY A SONG!

Goom'pa napped. The day's activities involving the rusty screw and Mauroga's rescue from the thunderstorm had left Goom'pa in a state of emotional and physical exhaustion.

"Groo!" Restless, Goom'pa stirred in his slumber. His teeny nostrils were flared.

In Goom'pa's dream, Bomboni chased him as he tried to make his escape after stealing a nut from the larger animal's lair. The squirrel closed the distance, appearing gigantic next to the Poofy.

Claws reached for Goom'pa's neck; he ran hard. The Poofy's tongue hung out, and he took rapid breaths...

Wide-eyed with fear, he sprinted, clasping the stolen nut.

Outraged, Bomboni bared sharp teeth and hissed. The distance narrowed and a paw tightened around Goom'pa's scrawny neck.

"Groo!" The Poofy let out a loud grunt and startled himself awake. Disoriented by the realistic vision, he felt his head reel.

"Groo, what a terrible dream!" Opening his eyes, Goom'pa focused on the thumb stuck in his mouth. The view made him cockeyed.

Upon realizing he was resting safe in the loft, his breathing slowed and softened. He climbed down and headed up and out of his underground home.

Peering outside, he scanned the night. The downpour had abated a while back, though scattered thunderheads still hung low. However, a breeze had stirred up, moving the heavy clouds quickly out of the area.

The rain-soaked soil smelt rich, and gloop circles glinted under the starlit sky.

Although the storm had raged strong over Miron National Forest, the showers had not fallen as hard in Palidon. This was due to the power of the magic spell.

Still, as he scurried to find a munchy, the Poofy kept his distance from the puddles scattered all over.

Famished, he snacked on a berry, nibbling on it with a light touch. The blueberry bush was still laden with gloop drops.

Finishing the delightful meal, he gazed up. From the position of the moon, Goom'pa knew midevening approached.

The tree cover and the remaining clouds blocked his view of Shine. Determined, Goom'pa decided to go to the meadow for an unobstructed vision of his love. On light feet, he waltzed his path, steering away from the moisture left over by the storm.

Shortly, he entered the clearing. A large gloop circle in the center caught his attention. Flowering plants surrounded the pooled water on all sides. Radiance emanated from it as if coming out of the earth itself!

Easing through the lush, damp blades of grass, Goom'pa hastened over to the pool. The moisture from the rainfall still clung to everything. Closer now, he paused.

Shine had shimmered with excitement when his stinky, furry form emerged into the pasture. With her celestial powers, she concentrated light rays on the pond. By focusing magic, her image shone strong on the water.

Goom'pa gazed into the perfect circular pond. *Groo*, it was so bright! A glow emanated, clear and strong. *What was the source of this crystal light*?

He leaned forward to peer closer into the liquid mirror.

"Groo!" Goom'pa yelped, seeing a vision in the gloop circle. Shine rested on top of the water, radiant and flawless.

Totally startled, Goom'pa jumped up in surprise and bumped his delicate head on a low-hanging branch.

Bonky!

The Poofy went down for the count. The world spun in slow circles as he tried to make sense of it all.

How had she come down to the meadow? He was overwhelmed by awe...and by the bump.

With a small sigh and a grunt, he passed out.

The princess suffered much love and confusion, looking down at her object of desire. "My Goom'pa, I adore you."

"What just happened?" she asked her friends.

"Your Poofy didn't understand he gazed at your reflection. Overwhelmed, he was startled and bumped his head!" explained the angels circling her.

"He needs help!" Shine brimmed with concern. Amid the flowering shrubs, her love lay prone from the bonky. Sprawled on the damp turf, he showed no sign of movement.

"Don't worry," her well-wishers assured the lovely princess. "Goom'pa shall be tended to!"

The heavenly spirits focused their minds and searched Palidon. They scanned, locking in on Shanista. The creature of the night perched high up on the oak, held vigil over the kingdom.

"Shanista!" Their collective voice entered her thoughts.

"Whoo, whoo? Who calls at this hour?" The owl breathed in the cool midnight scents.

"Oh, wise one, we're from lands far beyond. Please receive our adoration and our message."

"Whoo!" Shanista heard the song from above. In her mind's eye, she saw them clearly and experienced the events that had transpired.

The voices and visions vanished as suddenly as they had appeared.

Understanding her mission, she shot out of the tree and flew straight to the pasture. Gliding into the center, she arced under the sea-grape bush. Without slowing down, she picked up the still form with outstretched claws and swept out into the open.

Her powerful wings ate up the distance, as her sight pierced the shadows, choosing the best path despite the darkness.

"Ah, there it is!" The owl sensed her destination. With a sense of urgency, she sailed through the black of the jungle, carrying the frail creature.

Shortly, she alighted with a gentle touchdown and deposited the unconscious Goom'pa in the underbrush. His chest rose and fell in short breaths.

"Whoo, whoo!"

"Who's there?" A Poofy popped up from his cave-hole, looking sleepy.

"Whoo, Sadsak, your friend got a bonky!'

"Oh heavens, not again!" Sadsak scratched his scruff, straightening out his tuft.

"Please attend to him. Call for me if his situation doesn't improve."

"But of course, wise owl." Sadsak ran out with haste.

The darkness was still once more. Shanista had vanished.

"Groo, Goom'pa!" Sadsak cradled the patient's head in his lap. The doctor raised his poof, eyes shut tight, little body stiff. "Groooooo!" The Poofy cry went out.

Yes, this was beginning to unfold like a familiar scene.

Soon, the love-struck patient lay still on the matchbox once again with the "thermometer" sticking out through his whiskers. The doctor solemnly licked Goom'pa's bonky, to no avail.

D'uh, Plinka, and a few others had collected at the hospital. All looked on somberly.

"Ro-Ro." Sadsak was thoughtful.

"Yes, doc!"

"Blueberry." The plump Poofy shot off on the double and scurried back with a big, juicy one. But this time the munchy didn't do the trick!

Faces glum, the tiny animals surrounded the unconscious Poofy. They blinked at him, helpless.

Some scratching broke out. Sadsak appeared to be at his wits' end.

"Oh, Goom'pa!" The doctor was beside himself. "He goes about getting bonkies all the time, constantly up to mischief." Now, even the berry wasn't helping!

"Groo." Sadsak sighed, looking even smaller than usual.

"Whatever is that noise?" The group turned its attention to all of the commotion at SAH's entrance. And lo and behold, Plinka fell in through the opening!

No one had noticed him slip away. He returned now with his "harp." A moment of confusion and concern was followed by sheer terror. The others eyed Plinka nervously.

"Well, well, well. What, might I ask, is, err, going on?" Sadsak took a deep breath, desperately trying to maintain his composure.

With a determined expression, Plinka strolled over and sat down cross-legged next to the patient's bed. He appeared utterly puny but completely earnest. Without further delay, he began to strum the instrument and launched into a song.

"Eeee...aaaa...ooooo!" Plinka unleashed a long, mournful wail. The heartfelt cries would have put life into a dead cat.

The musical instrument had some history behind it.

The TV shows at the Varleys' residence influenced how the Poofys learned new things. Curious by nature, they tried to imitate the ways of the human world.

Plinka had discovered a red string in the Amazing Yellow Box.

Fascinated, he brought the item back to Palidon. The loot was bright and rare, but what should one do with it?

One day, he'd watched a particularly gripping TV show. On the show, one actor strummed a guitar; another played a cello. Now the Poofy wanted an instrument too!

A hunt was started for the frame of this new project. At last Ro-Ro came upon a bent twig that was the right size, about an inch long. He tied the red string to its ends so Plinka could pluck on it.

Thus, without quite intending, Ro-Ro had created a one-string harp for his friend. However, there was but a minor problem. No sound came of it.

None of the others had the heart to pass comment on this.

The musical device was brought out on special occasions. Unfortunately, Plinka began to sing along. The result was a terrible noise. Still, who would explain to him how they felt about the newfound talent?

And so, he plowed forth.

"Ooo...eee...aaaaaah!" He sang with passion, hitting lofty notes.

Ro-Ro had a haunted look in his wide eyes.

Sadsak gaped as if he would never smile ever again.

D'uh and the rest trembled under the assault upon their ears.

All did their best to resist the urge to flee SAH. Under no circumstance could they abandon the patient or hurt Plinka's feelings.

With a start, Goom'pa came alive and jumped half an inch high. He fell off the bed, raising a plume of magic powder, creating kneeshees among the group.

"What on earth is that sound!!?" Gingerly, he touched the tender bonky and gazed around, bewildered.

The earnest cries had penetrated Goom'pa's hearing.

The tiny musician's face cracked into a toothy smile. "I play for you! I do," he plucked happily.

"Oh, wow!" By now Goom'pa, though shaken, was wary and very much awake.

"Yours is quite a talent there, dear Plinka. Please, take a rest!"

The others nodded in desperate agreement.

In a flash of inspiration, Ro-Ro pulled out a couple of delicious sunflower seeds from Sadsak's stash and deposited them in front of the musician's dainty paw-feet.

"I sing later?" He held on tightly to the harp, inquiring with a soulful look.

"Yes, yes! Later!" agreed the others, vigorously shaking their poofs.

"Please rest for a bit. The song has spread good cheer to many," begged Ro-Ro.

"Groo, and brought our friend back to life." D'uh nodded.

Goom'pa stared at Plinka with a stony eye, biting his tongue.

Plinka nibbled daintily on the seeds. Satisfied for the time being, he seemed to believe his work was done here.

The others gave their adventurous friend a pat on his shoulder and a quick licky on his bonky. The bump was calming down already.

Seizing the moment, the group of friends erupted into a stampede for the exit before Plinka changed his mind.

The love-struck Poofy told Sadsak his story. The doctor sighed and rolled his eyes. He gave Goom'pa a pat and sent him on his way.

Goom'pa recovered rapidly, making skippies through the night. The gloop circles were almost gone as the fertile forest soil absorbed the rains.

"Your treasured one is doing well. Favored by the gods, he will be fine." Zydaar had returned to update the princess.

"Thank you, dear guardian." Elated, Shine nodded her gratitude and sighed with longing for her love.

Her object of adoration crawled back into his dwelling, tired. There had been a lot of activity, a packed day, even for this busy soul.

As he slowly walked to the rear of the tunnel, he absent-mindedly played with his poof. He checked the offerings accumulated for his Shine.

The peanut, yes, it was there. It had begun to smell a bit.

"Groo, the Golden Cone." Filled with pride, Goom'pa scampered over and caressed the rusty screw with a delicate paw.

How he would impress her with these fancy gifts. Goom'pa gave the treasure a careful licky.

With a contented grunt, he climbed back up to the loft. As sleep took over, he returned to dreamland.

14

SHINE STAR—THE SOLUTION

Prime was thoughtful.

He knew now which direction to take. After his consultation with the Elanians, the solution had emerged.

The choice was between the life he wanted for Shine and the one that would bring her true happiness. Though he didn't doubt anymore, his heart was heavy.

"Young princess."

"Daddy!" She heard his call.

"No father can rest in peace while his child lacks joy and suffers. What shall make you happy once again?" Yes, he'd already reached a conclusion, but having Shine's say on the subject was important.

"Always, you are good to me." Eyes full of adoration, she gave a small smile. While Prime Ray observed her twinkling far away, in his inner vision she sparkled with even more clarity.

"Papa, I understand what's right and meant to fulfill me. Further, I see this as the ideal choice because Goom'pa's innocence is deeply precious. It wouldn't be fair to turn his world upside down."

Hence, she explained to her father that she would descend to Palidon. She must appeal to magic and the powers of the Elanians to help her in this quest.

"With every fiber of my being, I yearn to live in this land of sweetness with Goom'pa. To uproot this untouched soul from his natural environment would cause much confusion and potential harm to him. That would hardly be an act of kind-ness!" She spoke passionately.

"You know, Daddy, there is no escaping the simple conclu-sion. All other choices would prove selfish."

His heart hurt, yet he couldn't obstruct her happiness. He would now have to determine next steps. Prime Ray was grate-ful to be father to such a divine energy.

He faded from her thoughts.

On the far end of the void, billions of miles away, ruled the Red Giant, Rath.

Black storms raged through his restless form. Over the years, his strength had increased steadily. In addition to the Milky Way, he commanded countless other galaxies and further mag-nificent formations.

With a strong hand, he exercised authority, quick to use his powers when faced with obstacles.

Relentless, Rath marched ever toward glory. Formidable, he hadn't emerged as a dominant force over the ages by act-ing impulsively. Displaying unerring judgment and the mental strength required to oversee widespread territories, the giant forged ahead.

Yet he had a master, king of the manifest universe, Prime Ray.

The relationship prospered based on mutual need and admi-ration. A leader as strong as Rath wouldn't accept another's au-thority with ease. He was shrewd enough, however, to respect the strength of the king and the other Star Lords.

Having the ability to be patient and judicious in his choice of moves, Rath erected a vast empire. Among the chiefs, he raised caution and fear. However, they, for their part, hadn't attained enormous might by being easily intimidated. In watchful fashion, Rath wielded muscle over sweeping territories in the limitless ocean of space. Always, he remained careful and crafty in his dealings with others in power.

An uneasy truce prevailed among the five chiefs. Most of the time, they exercised reason and managed their own egos well. These titans ensured that the countless entities and creatures inhabiting the kingdoms didn't pay the foolish price of a war of vanity between them.

Under Prime Ray's sway, better sense usually won out.

"Relangaa, greetings and a dispatch for Lord Rath." Megalon swept in with a flurry of orange sparks.

"Hail, old comrade! What hastens you to these parts, Megalon?"

One of Rath's generals, Relangaa was also his first in command, an Ancient. Along with Mauroga, he had been assigned and pledged to help the chief to reign with wisdom.

"Master, a messenger arrives."

The Red Giant was brooding over an issue of conflict concerning Ba'raan. The two chiefs butted heads often over endless years.

Rath raised an eyebrow.

"Megalon brings compliments from his lord, and a request."

Prime had once more reached out to him. And so, the meeting was arranged.

"Hail, Rath!" The ruler entered his awareness.

"How can I be of assistance?"

"We reviewed a particular matter with you thousands of years ago." The emperor reminded him of their discussion about a star named Sun, its planet Earth, and of an enchanted place called Palidon.

Silent, Rath looked within and searched his memories. *Ah! The elfin kingdom.*

"Upon your request, the region has been surrounded by a Magic Protection Spell cast by the Elanians," Rath agreed.

"Your memory serves you well."

"You're kind, Prime Ray. I'm reminded of Mauroga. Do tell, how may I help you this time?"

"My child, Shine Star, desires to descend and live out her life on Earth, in Palidon. This is her wish. The demand isn't put forth casually," explained Prime.

"Your daughter won't be an Eternal anymore?" This meeting and entreaty were highly unusual.

Prime Ray let it be known that this was true.

"Shine can never go back to living as a supernatural. She must submit to the Laws of Free Will. Is this price to be paid?" Rath asked, astonished.

Again, Prime Ray answered that this was the case. "You can imagine, this isn't an easy choice for me. But I would have Shine live a brief life of love rather than spend an eternity in misery. This needs to be done."

"Very well." Rath rumbled a low growl. "You do then appreciate the courtesy I ask for in return. It is my duty to consult with the Elanian fairies before giving any formal assent. It takes a lot to surprise me, but this involves your youngster, Shine. Hence, I shall not comment any further now."

Prime Ray agreed. "Please go ahead and confer with the wise ones. But do me the favor of a prompt response. You have my gratitude in advance," echoed the king's voice as he withdrew.

Trying to make sense of the new developments, Rath spent much time reviewing the exchange.

Hmmm, might this be an attempt at deception? He frowned hard.

Would the king risk his own child for a power play of some kind? Deep red eyes swirled with raging storms.

Meanwhile, Relangaa hovered nearby awaiting any directives. He knew his chief had communicated with Prime Ray regarding something serious.

"Ancient one."

"Master."

"Go, petition Istara for an audience. Her advice is required on an urgent subject."

Relangaa rode star-beams, traveling halfway across the realm.

The Elanians were joined in a circle. As one, they sang a song of divine love. Upon arrival, Relangaa felt the chimes resonate through his frame. Sweet harmonies in the hymn, the fairies wove a delicate spell to correct energy imbalances in the heavens.

Their sound judgment made them a trusted source of advice to the masters of the universe. Of course, those powerful titans didn't always heed the counsel they asked for.

Patiently, the visitor knelt and waited.

The song came to a sweet end. For a moment, Istara remained in prayer. Finally, she cast a kind glance at Relangaa.

"Speak, Ancient One." Her voice was but a whisper.

With urgency, he conveyed his master's request for advice. The fairy had been expecting this and was prepared.

"Fond greetings!" She made instant contact with Rath.

"Dear Istara, I'm grateful to you for your kind attention. What must I make of these demands?" He told her of the king's visit and the unexpected appeal.

"Is this a trap of some sort kind set by Prime?" He knew the Elanians might choose not to answer every question. If Istara hesitated, that would warn him he had cause for concern.

"This is a solely a matter for Shine's happiness. In this, her father doesn't have an agenda. In fact, he's in distress over her wishes."

"Does Prime Ray fully fathom she will lose her everlasting and divine powers?"

"Indeed."

"Well, my questions are satisfied, and your generous advice is appreciated." Rath retreated from her consciousness.

Istara sighed deeply. She hadn't lied to Rath or misled him. She wouldn't do so. However, she hadn't told him of Goom'pa and Shine's tenderness for each other. "Ambitious Rath wouldn't be able to fathom this sacred sentiment," she told her closest ones. "It would confuse him and might lead to the turning down of Prime's request." Upon review, Istara felt her answers had been direct.

"Should Rath obstruct the king, extreme unrest will follow, with ill effects for the inhabitants of the entire cosmos," she mused.

The Red Giant had asked, and Istara had given him an appropriate response.

Voicing her hopes, she fervently prayed for the Poofy and his princess.

15

GOOM'PA—HOP-SKIPPIES
WITH FRIENDS

By early evening in Palidon, the shadows had grown long. A light breeze began to kick up from the east.

Meanwhile, the sun sank slowly in the west, to rest for the late hours.

The Poofys didn't know where the golden ball went for sleep. After dusk, he disappeared for the night behind the Varley house. Like a charm, he arose on the other side every day. He was quite regular in his habits.

"Groo...how does he do that?" Goom'pa marveled on occasion, but the thought was much too complicated and made him do scratchies.

The yellow, shimmering orb slipped away over the western horizon to his nightly resting place.

Dusk approached, cooling the woods.

Goom'pa, Ro-Ro, and D'uh were playing hop-skippies, a game popular with the Poofys. The little creatures liked to have fun; the simpler the pastime, the better.

All paws planted on the magic powder, Ro-Ro bent over. "Groo!" Each time he leaned over, he grunted.

About a foot ahead of him, D'uh also bowed over, limbs pressed into the ground. As a result of all the play and activity, his dented tuft wore a sprinkling of dirt.

A twinkle in his eye, Goom'pa rushed toward Ro-Ro. His front paws made contact with the Poofy's back, which catapulted Goom'pa over the pudgy frame.

With a toothy grin, he sailed through the air, poof swaying in the breeze.

Touching down nimbly, Goom'pa seamlessly launched into more hops. Next thing, he was upon D'uh.

Rewind and repeat. Landing lightly on his tiny playmate's back, he soared away.

Ah, what fun!

Creating distance between D'uh and himself, Goom'pa bent over, breathing hard. His small, furry form was warm from the exertion.

Up next was Ro-Ro. Despite his best efforts, he didn't quite skip. The well-fed body wobbled and jiggled as he ambled sluggishly in D'uh's direction. As Ro-Ro prepared for a third attempt, his mouth hung open from the strain.

Yes, he was tiring quickly.

Meanwhile, D'uh shut his eyes. He braced himself for his friend's bulk, which came lumbering toward him.

Upon arrival, Ro-Ro kind of staggered onto his pal. As he placed chubby paws on D'uh's back, he burped. The plump creature then attempted to launch his mass.

For a moment, he rose, not quite airborne, and then sank heavy atop his playmate. A plume of dust erupted. Neither could be seen for a bit.

Another burp!

"Chooee...! Chooee!" D'uh had the kneeshees.

In haste, the two Poofys scrambled up. Covered completely in magic powder, they looked like tiny ghosts. Straightening up, Goom'pa stared at the spectacle. His whiskers twitched with emotion.

A wide-eyed Ro-Ro was clearly embarrassed. D'uh and he stood there exchanging looks. The smaller fellow stroked his poof.

Soulfully, they scoped each other.

"Groo, groo, ha, ha, ha!" Without warning, they both broke into toothy smiles and much laughter.

"Groo, groo!" Chuckling out loud, Goom'pa gamboled over, a big grin on his impish face.

That was enough for today. Dusk was sweeping in, and the early stars had begun to reveal themselves. The three pals parted for the evening.

Headed for a clump of raspberry bushes, Goom'pa did a little dance. The activity had left him thirsty and hungry, and he yearned for a plump and ripe red munchy.

Along the path, he stopped and sniffed the blossoms. He spoke to the bees making their way home laden with nectar from beautiful blooms that offered their bounty so generously.

Goom'pa reached his destination an hour later, having taken his time. Famished, he clambered up a large bush with haste and tugged urgently on a ripe treat. It wouldn't give. He examined the raspberry intently.

"Mmm!" He smacked his lips, drooling and wanting for the juicy delight.

A smart little Poofy, he swung from the branch. Arm stretched, he reached out and clutched the stem, wrapping his body around the munchy. In a lazy rhythm, he began to swing to and fro. The fruit broke free and fell to the ground as he held on.

Upon landing nimbly in the lush underbrush, Goom'pa rolled away and thus avoided creating a mess by squishing the prize. After resting briefly, he made a merry feast on the plump fruit.

"Groo." Wiping sticky whiskers, the little fellow ate with delight.

Soon, he relaxed on his back, soft tummy tight and full. Sweet juices covered his face and he licked his paws to savor every last morsel of the delicious meal.

"Burppp! Groo...groo! Thank you. That was yum!"

"Most welcome, my dear friend. The treats are but to be shared. Your enjoyment and gratitude begins much pleasure." The bush swayed gently.

The dark had arrived. In the dim light, Goom'pa scanned the forest. High above, the stars shone as if liquid silver. Goom'pa sat up straight. Cloudy weather had prevented a clear view of his sweet angel for the last two days.

On playful feet, he pranced through the thick vegetation. The woods appeared magical and luminous under the rising moon. On his way to the Meadow of Flowers, Goom'pa abruptly changed direction. Not as shy of Shine any more, he hustled to the Dome to be closer to his love.

His tummy ached. The Poofy missed the princess so.

Upon emerging into the opening, Goom'pa bounded up the incline on all fours. He sat down and searched the skies.

There. She sparkled—an angelic star, gleaming, like a diamond on fire.

"Shine Star." Goom'pa reached out to his heart and joy.

From afar, she gazed down on Palidon, picking up his feelings.

"Groo, Shine!" Her sweet creature looked up. The princess reflected in his eyes. They widened with love.

"My Goom'pa!"

"I missed you...couldn't sight you for two darks!"

"Precious Poofy, but I'm always here."

"Groo?"

"Yes?"

"Groo...why I long for you all the time? Groo...how come I pine for you, even while making munchy and crunchy?"

"My love, I miss you too, every moment. Expect a personal note from me. May it bring you much joy." She gleamed with delight at the tiny form.

"Groo, groo...how I get these words?"

"They shall be conveyed by someone you know."

"Groo, I have presents for you. I give to this one?"

"Yes, please do hand them over to the messenger. I await them with much eagerness!" She radiated hugs.

"Groo...OK! I go now to get the gifts!"

With every ounce of concentration, Goom'pa planted his whiskers on the grass. After kissing the ground several times, he scurried away into the darkness.

And the kisses bloomed.

The call went out!

"Smackoos, to be collected!" Vinorgaan and the Glitonian Sparkles streaked across the firmament.

It was another busy night in paradise.

✳ ✳ ✳

16

RATH—THE PLAN

Under Prime's oversight, they ruled the universe.

Ba'raan. Mir'om. Sarvithos, Vanthisar and Rath. Five formidable Star Lords.

Of them, Rath was matchless in drive and ambition, the one whom the other chiefs feared.

The descent of Shine to Palidon would happen soon. Rath reflected on the ruler's mood when their minds had engaged, his sense of urgency in attempting to resolve his daughter's dilemma.

Whatever should he make of all this? To allow one's own young to be reduced to a mere mortal on a whimsy? What exactly was this indulgence? In hindsight, Rath realized he hadn't asked about Shine's motivations.

Deep in thought, he tried to make sense of the developments. Now, a plan birthed.

Over the eons, Prime Ray focused tirelessly on managing the kingdoms. All the while, he maintained supreme authority, juggling the balance of power among the lords. There was good reason why he endured as Ruler of All, Rath acknowledged.

However, during their exchange, had Rath picked up on weakness? The other chiefs, meanwhile, remained unaware of Shine's impending journey.

If ever, Rath saw an opportunity here.

With a move at the right moment, he could attack Prime. The others wouldn't see it coming. By the time they reacted, it would be too late.

Yet, danger lurked, Rath mused. Should he fail, Prime would bring Rath to his knees. He risked total destruction. Although, done right, he could take swift control of the kingdoms. He would emerge as the king.

This was the opening he had waited for! His being raced with excitement as he contemplated strategy.

"Relangaa."

"Lord Rath." The Red Angel swooped in.

"Fetch Mauroga."

The Ancient sped away.

Relangaa entered the green planet's atmosphere. Suspended over Palidon, he turned on his cloak of invisibility.

"Purple Angel." Relangaa reached out.

"Old friend, what brings you to this humble domain? It's good to set eyes on you after many ages." The jaguar transformed and appeared before Relangaa in his natural state. Mauroga, in Ancient form, pulsed with intense lights.

The two enjoyed mutual company for a while.

"You, too, look good!" The visitor shone with a red intensity reflected off of silver wings. "I come with urgency. Rath summons you in utmost secrecy."

Upon hearing the command, Mauroga kept any reservations to himself. In an instant, the two angels were off.

✳ ✳ ✳

Rath surfaced from his thoughts. His two stalwarts hovered in front of him.

"Trusted Mauroga, welcome. We need your counsel on a critical matter."

Mauroga bowed his head in respect. "It is my honor. What troubles Rath so deeply?"

"Relangaa, stay. I seek advice from both of you."

The two waited.

"Hear me with care." Their master spoke bluntly. "I sense weakness and confusion in Prime Ray. In my opinion, such failings are not desirable in one who is the king of the universe.

"Hence, I plan to move swiftly and wrest supremacy from him."

The Ancients listened, intently to every word.

Rath might be successful in this endeavor, but at a price. Massive devastation and loss of life would occur. Thousands of years, if not more, would pass before the chaos that ensued subsided.

"I have ideas to present you for advice. Before I get into details, let me have your initial response to my decision." Rath waited.

Their duty remained to provide guidance yet not interfere. In balance, the Eternal would only be truly strong if the free will of the masters of the universe wasn't tampered with.

What counsel must Relangaa give? Troubled, his thoughts raced. The cosmos was about to be hit by a hurricane. He couldn't stand in the way, by oath.

Mauroga reacted much more quickly. Rath's ambitions were not secret. What did surprise the Ancient was his own response. Assessing the urgency of the situation, he wasted no time.

"You ask for advice. The matter is as grave as any you have conferred with me on. So indulge me as I offer the following."

Rath stared back with red eyes, attentive. Though the ultimate decision rested in his hands, he held Mauroga in the highest regard.

The Purple Angel knelt in the vast blackness. "Please accept these." Two glistening thought-balls emerged from his head.

The Red Giant nodded his assent and the shining orbs glided up to him. He took in the first shimmering sphere. What happened next unfolded in seconds.

As if he had been present, Rath witnessed the story of Mauroga's descent into Palidon and the Magic Protection Bubble that the fairies wove with powerful charm. Over endless years, the Ancient, Mauroga came to know and became attached to the inhabitants of this mystical land. As their protector, he watched over them.

More images rushed by, showing the tenderness he'd developed for the Poofys and how the jaguar was humbled by the deep bonds these souls shared, their trust in one another and their world.

Rath felt greatly unsettled by his own reactions.

He then accepted the second sphere. Thus, he experienced Shine Star's essence, the miracle of her creation, her loving intelligence, and the delight she took in all beings. He witnessed the joy she took in Goom'pa and the simple wisdom of his heart; how the princess and the creature became conscious of each other; and the sweet, happy lives of the Poofys.

Unexpected sentiments boiled up in Rath as he continued.

He saw the love the princess and the Poofy shared. Rath sensed their mutual longing.

He came to appreciate the king's humility in coming to him and seeking special protection for Palidon. He better understood the qualities that made Prime Ray the ruler that he was.

Rath erupted in violent storms and raging fires. These were an expression of the conflict in his core.

The visions of the story of Shine and Goom'pa raced through his consciousness, penetrating deep into his very soul.

The Ancient Ones waited, circling him for a long time.

Calm returned after the storm.

Finally, Rath focused on the Ancients. A curious emotion lurked in his eyes.

"Mauroga." Rath's voice was quiet but strong.

"Yes?"

"You are wise."

"My lord."

"And we are grateful to you. Please return to your post."

The angel complied and departed.

In a split second, the jaguar was back in Palidon, resting high up. Having fulfilled his duty, he returned to keeping an eye on the forest residents.

17

SHINE STAR—THE GIFTS

Zydaar appeared before the princess and received her communication. "It shall be done," he responded.

He soared off to Palidon. Upon arrival, he cloaked his form.

The jaguar sensed the approach and changed form. Silently he approached the new arrival. The two knelt before each other. Brothers in a sacred order, assigned different masters, they had a mutual bond and shared respect that remained strong.

"Greetings, Mauroga."

"Welcome, Zydaar. I am somewhat surprised to see you here."

"I carry a dispatch from our precious Shine for a popular inhabitant of this enchanted land."

Mauroga listened with rapt attention to every word.

"Shine Star will shortly descend to unite with her cherished Goom'pa."

Solemnly, Mauroga received the message. Absorbing its impact, he shook his head, astonished. "The princess chooses to give up rights as an Eternal? Prime and Rath give consent to this plan?"

In response Zydaar communicated recent events to Mauroga, including the intricacies of the recent meeting between Rath and Prime Ray.

"Good heavens!" Over countless years, Mauroga had witnessed incredible events unfold. Yet he was astonished and moved by this particular tale.

"What needs to be done?"

"With your permission, I will wait here. Meanwhile, would you please convey the news to the Poofy? I also believe he has tributes for our princess. If you could deliver them to me, I intend to be on my way."

"But of course. I shall return soon." A jaguar again, Mauroga melted into the shadows.

In stealth, he closed upon the cave-hole.

"Goom'pa!" he rumbled, crouching beside the sea-grape bush.

There was no response. The Poofy wasn't home.

Wait! Someone approached on playful little feet.

"That whiff." Mauroga picked up a familiar scent.

Goom'pa came to a stop, watchful eyes spotting Mauroga near the entrance to his shelter. "Groo?"

"Yes, young Poofy."

"Groo, what brings you here? I am busy tonight."

"I understand. I bring a message and believe you have an offering in return." The cat regarded him with a searching look.

"Ya! Are you the message person?" Goom'pa skipped up to him, jumped high, and tugged on the huge cat's whiskers. The jaguar waited patiently for the little one to calm down.

"Yes, that's correct. The princess sends the following words: 'My love, I find it increasingly unbearable to be without you anymore. On the eve of the full moon, I will descend from the heavens. Forever, we are to make happy skippies together!'" Thus spoke Mauroga.

Overjoyed, Goom'pa ran around the messenger in circles and jumped on the big feline's back, bouncing up and down with glee.

"Groo, groo! Shine is coming to Palidon!" In a tizzy, he was all toothy grins and joy itself.

The protector waited in calm silence while the Poofy digested the news.

"The hours pass, and we must be quick. Please let me collect the gifts for Shine, as I cannot stay here much longer."

Like a shot, the little one was off Mauroga's back and disappeared into the cave-hole. A few moments later, he popped out, covered with dirt and carrying something. Then he retreated, returning with something heavier. Breathing hard, he struggled over to the big cat with the presents. The jaguar squinted, trying to pierce the blackness.

"Groo!" Goom'pa gazed at the cat with moist brown eyes.

The Ancient extended a massive paw. Goom'pa heaved and grunted, placing two articles on it.

"And, umm, these are for me to cart back?" The protector inspected them. A rotting peanut and a rusty screw rested on his giant paw.

"Yes, don't just stand around, you growly cat. Go now. Please take them to my Shine!"

The sleek shadow slipped into the jungle.

"I give thanks, Mauroga," Zydaar told his fellow angel. "The princess offers gratitude and blessings for your assistance." As

Mauroga's old friend beheld the objects, he tried to keep a straight face.

"It is but my pleasure."

The two treated the gifts with utmost care and respect.

The guest sped away, a shooting star in a sea of blackness.

Moments later, Shine giggled with delight upon his arrival with the presents.

"Oh, Zydaar." While she didn't relate to the form of the presents, her being soaked in the innocence contained in the offerings.

In joy, she radiated bright. The universe rejoiced with her. Brilliant rays crisscrossed the heavens.

Soon she would be on her way to Earth and to her beloved.

18

RATH—THE
TRANSFORMATION

"Relangaa, trusted one."

"Yes?" Deeply unsettled, the Ancient knelt. He had been present when the Purple Angel had given consultation to their master.

"Please go to Prime Ray. Request a private audience."

"Sire." The angel took off.

"A pleasant surprise." Megalon reached out to welcome Relangaa on his arrival. "What brings you here with such haste?"

"Rath requests an urgent personal meeting."

The Orange Angel delivered the communication to the king.

"Of course, I shall convene with Rath immediately."

The assent was passed on. And almost right away, the king felt Rath's presence.

"Greetings, Rath. What troubles you?" As the two engaged, Prime couldn't recall ever observing the Red Giant in so anxious a mood.

"May I?" Rath floated a thought-ball to him.

The king hid his surprise. The powerful chief had never revealed his thoughts on such an intimate basis before. Was this a trick? Focusing on the shining sphere, Prime didn't read danger or misguided intent.

"Why, of course." He viewed the incredible story offered up to him, of the emergence of a young and ambitious star with a ruthless desire to succeed; of how, as his empire grew, the happier he had hoped to be; and of his complicated relationship with the king.

Initially, the young star had a subconscious longing to re-place the emperor. Then the ambition surfaced as a conscious idea.

Presently, he saw his chance.

He summoned Mauroga.

The Red Giant became enlightened about Goom'pa and Shine. He came to appreciate the wisdom of the Poofys. The quest for power would never afford Rath the simple joys and pleasures the creatures of Palidon already experienced.

The will to rule and conquer was broken.

Strong and courageous Rath. The king was amazed. It took a big and brave heart to share such innermost thoughts.

"Prime Ray, please hear me out! You now understand what I intended. The plan was to destroy you and take over the em-pires. However, having absorbed the stories shared with me, I cannot," explained Rath.

"I realize now, the universe needs the wisdom of your rule. No more do I deem myself fit to be a commander. I formally ab-dicate status as a chief and am willing to face the consequences for all intent and actions." Rath humbled himself.

"Slow down, my friend!" responded Prime Ray. "The king-doms call upon your strength, now more than ever." Prime viewed Rath with marvel and respect.

"You have emerged the mightiest of commanders. The boundless ambition and hunger are balanced by a capacity to exercise profound judgment. With your recent transformation and the courage to share it, you emerge a true and wise leader. Accept my hand of friendship. Together, let's protect what is precious." Prime Ray pulsed with admiration.

"My king, I am to be by your side. The gracious gift you bestow upon me is an undeserved honor." In that moment, Rath knew humility. "I do have one favor to call for."

"Ask. What is it that Lord Rath desires?"

"I want to ensure Shine Star's descent into this special land is showered with the sweetness and grace the passage deserves." Such was Rath's generous petition to his king.

"With great joy, Red Giant, I do receive your affection!"

There followed a rich exchange of feelings between the two immortals.

A ripple of joy passed through the fabric of creation.

＊

19

GOOM'PA AND SHINE—
THE CELEBRATION

The Elanian Council circled Shine. They sang of love.

Thousands of Glitonian Sparkles flew in, amid much excitement. Around Earth, they formed a rainbow ring of multicolored lights. With squeals of delight, they danced and twirled. Vinorgaan watched over them, assisted by a team of helpers.

Cutting through the Elanian chants, Istara lifted her voice. With a tone crystal pure, her prayer rang across the heavens.

At Rath's insistence, his vast armies coordinated arrangements for the celestial celebration. Under his supervision, angels and fairies of a thousand orders had assembled.

At regular intervals, they lined the way, paving a path of shimmering lights. The bridge extended billions of miles, from Shine Star to the Milky Way, Sun, and Earth.

These heavenly beings, this complex network of magical entities, had diverse assignments in countless galaxies and stellar systems. With vigilance and dedication, they ensured the whole universe ran optimally. The Red Giant had coordinated with the chiefs to call upon their resources on this, most special, of days.

The Star Lords and the king, they all present. Surrounding the princess with their commanding energies, they murmured ancient hymns, creating auspicious vibrations.

A rare, if ever, meeting of the most powerful minds.

In unison and amity...

Istara's clear voice rang out far, filling every corner of the cosmos.

The Glitonians began to spin faster around Earth, with much laughter and delight.

This elaborate spectacle could not be seen by humans but was visible to the dwellers of Palidon. The festivities were meant to honor Shine and Goom'pa!

The millions of spirits lining the path from the princess's abode in the heavens to the green planet knelt upon hearing Istara. They unfurled their magnificent wings, made of stardust and webs of light. Their radiance fused together, creating a crystalline pathway.

The bridge extended forever. The path led all the way to Palidon. This blinding arc of silver, infinitely long, was seen only by divine beings and residents of the enchanted forest.

As Istara summoned powerful blessings, the universe overflowed with joy. And something in creation changed. In that instant, peace reigned everywhere.

Where a bloody battle was being waged, the warriors felt an unusual empathy for their so-called enemies. Exhaustion overtook them, and they realized they had lost the will to fight. Many took a nap; others took a break and wandered around aimlessly.

No one clashed in the streets or schools. A bully crowded over a child he had cornered. An odd emotion swept over him as he looked into the little boy's frightened eyes. Reaching out uncertainly, he gave the kid a pat on the head. Both stumbled away, confused.

A hunter had a deer in his sights. The mountain air was brisk. As his finger put light pressure on the trigger, he centered his scope on the target. Hesitating at the last minute, he experienced deep tenderness for the gentle creature. The man lowered his rifle and snuck on gloves to warm his frozen hands. A bit befuddled by his reaction, he wandered away.

Istara's chant rang out, pure, stirring every conscious entity.

A thousand varieties of celestial spirits responded in myriad ways to join the festivities. The path forged to the Milky Way by the angels' wings lit up and glowed.

The Ancient Ones formed a circle around Shine to escort her—all except the fierce Mauroga, who waited below.

With Shanista's help, Cheenoo, Ro-Ro's wife, had taken care of all the arrangements, and the Poofys gathered in the Meadow of Flowers.

The jaguar stood to the left of the love-struck, but always stinky, Goom'pa. Ro-Ro, Plinka, D'uh, and Sadsak were to his right, with the others grouped behind them.

Wide-eyed, Goom'pa waited for his princess, this eve of the full moon.

The Poofys had given each other a lick-down. They stood proud, oily and shiny. Their poofs glistened under the moon, which beamed extra bright in the twilight.

Bomboni headed a party of squirrels that looked a little cleaner and sleeker for the event. A large number of forest animals with close ties to the Poofys had turned out. All were gathered in fairly good order and surveyed the night skies.

There appeared an arc of crystal white light. It streaked over the eastern horizon and down into the pasture. The heavens lit up.

The dazzling blooms in the clearing swayed.

All Poofys showed a hint of red sparkle in their tufts. Something fancy had to be done to welcome Shine Star!

Earlier, Cheenoo consulted with Shanista, and Mauroga had assisted. The jaguar arranged for the owl to be allowed beyond the Magic Protection Bubble.

In silence, she had swooped into the Varley house at dusk. After snooping around, she discovered shiny red packing paper in one of the rooms.

Buddy barked furiously. Had he heard movement in the master bedroom? With a growl, he leapt up to check.

Emma "shushed" him as they ate dinner. But he bounded up the stairs and into the chambers. A closet door creaked as it swung open. As he burst upon the scene, a flash of white flew out a window that was ajar.

On guard, Mauroga crouched nearby, watching the cottage. Shanista's mission proved successful!

The prize was duly delivered to Cheenoo and the other girl Poofys. Excited, they quickly bit into it and tore the treasure up into a hundred glossy little pieces.

And so, Ro-Ro had stood at attention, his tongue hanging out, eyes wide open. Cheenoo had given him strict instructions not to move. The others Poofys formed a line in front of him and waited.

As each stepped forward, Cheenoo slapped a tiny red piece of paper across Ro-Ro's wet tongue, and firmly stuck the decoration on each poof.

Goom'pa was also ready, with a high poof today! The little fellow held a juicy blueberry in his paws. He had licked it clean with much care.

Shanista was perched on Mauroga's right shoulder.

As the angels unfolded the bridge of light, the Ancients surrounding Shine Star merged their minds.

The journey for the princess could have taken countless years. Momentarily, the Lords of Time joined hands with the forces of the supernatural, folding time into a spinning ball. The actual trip would take but a minute.

Shine had been waiting for just this moment. Her heart danced, and she glowed.

Ever faithful, Zydaar knelt before her. Leaving her abode of light, Shine swooped in and rested on his palm. He turned around, pointing the way to her destination.

The procession began. Others followed, heads bowed in honor. The party of heavenly beings descended the bridge of starlight.

The Star Lords and their king viewed the celebrations.

Prime was not in pain today. He felt no hurt in the knowledge of the occasion. Shine was in bliss. She had the opportunity to experience perfect, innocent love.

Rath followed the events quietly, enveloped in a newfound calm, a serenity he had never known before.

Thus, Shine arrived in Palidon.

Just before entering, she glanced back.

She offered her father warmth and gratitude. To forsake eternity for love, ever pure, he had granted his creation this freedom.

To every angel and fairy, Shine expressed joy—to the young Glitonians, the Ancients, the Elanians, the shooting stars, her playmates, and more.

To the graceful spirits that lined the path to her new home, she radiated hugs.

Holding his gigantic face in her hands, she kissed her guardian on his nose. "Is the mighty Zydaar blushing?" She giggled.

The princess sailed into Palidon, gliding through the Magic Protection Bubble. On light feet, she touched ground in the Meadow of Flowers.

In that instant, Shine was transformed. She emerged as a dainty white Poofy with a wavy dark-brown tuft! With a toothy grin, she smiled at the heavens.

The Ancients bowed and departed.

The Glitonians laughed lightly and sped away.

The silver arc formed by the angels glowed brilliantly. Then, it was gone.

The divine forces retreated to their natural order and place in the cosmos. The Star Lords withdrew to focus on their kingdoms.

Prime Ray sent out blessings, having come to truly understand what gave meaning to the living, breathing universe.

The princess gazed adoringly at her sweet Poofy...

Goom'pa gawked!

In his haste, he dropped the blueberry and almost tripped over it, scampering toward her. Luckily, the shiny red paper stuck to his scruff!

In joy, she made skippies and did somersaults.

He ran up to her. They held each other.

Her object of desire went cross-eyed, seeing Shine's whiskers so close up.

Uttering a low growl, Mauroga slowly walked away into the dark woods.

Shanista's piercing gray vision sent blessings to the new Poofy pair. With a flutter of wings, she took off from the cat's shoulder and flew for the shadows.

Bomboni snatched the fallen berry, hastily gulped it down, and scampered off.

Cheenoo stood on her toes and gave Ro-Ro's nose a licky, making him blush!

Under the glittering full moon, in the midst of the luminescent and lustrous flowers that had opened for the night, they all made munchies on treats gathered for the feast.

Goom'pa and Shine stopped playing for a moment.

The princess's white fur was already covered with magic powder. Beautiful brown eyes gazed at Goom'pa. He looked back shyly and did some nervous scratchies.

With dainty soft paws, she reached out to hold his face. And she gave him a kissy.

Overcome with joy, Goom'pa ran around in circles.

A game of hop-skippies broke out.

They partied till dawn.

Shine had come to Palidon. All was well with the universe.

At least for now...

✳ ✳ ✳

NOTE TO THE READER:

I hope you enjoyed Goom'pa and Shine. I would encourage you to take a moment and visit Amazon.com to post a favorable comment.

Your support will go a long way in promoting indie publishing!

Vikrant Malhotra has always enjoyed creating his own worlds with pen and paper. After dabbling in children's novels, he recently published his first book, *The Stories of Goom'pa: Book One*.

Malhotra is currently hard at work on a sequel that leads Goom'pa and Shine to new adventures and surprises.